* * * * * * *

As soon as he had everything he needed on his horse, and his horse was ready to travel, Jake went into the barn and found the can of coal oil his father kept to use in the lanterns. He took it to the cabin and splashed some of it inside the cabin and the rest over the front of the cabin. Jake stepped back and said a short prayer his mother had taught him as a child, then vowed to find and kill the men who had murdered his parents.

He took a match, lit it and set the cabin on fire. Jake stood in front of the cabin and watched as the flames quickly spread engulfing the entire cabin. The heat from the flames matched the heated anger he felt in his heart.

* * * * * * *

Other titles by J.E. Terrall

Western Short Stories	Western Novels
The Old West*	Conflict in Elkhorn Valley*
The Frontier*	Lazy A Ranch
Untamed Land*	(A Modern Western)
Tales from the Territory*	The Story of Joshua Higgins*
Frontier Justice*	The Valley Ranch War*
Jake Murdock, Bounty Hunter*	

Romance Novels	Mystery/Suspense/Thriller
Balboa Rendezvous	I Can See Clearly*
Sing for Me*	The Return Home*
Return to Me*	The Inheritance
Forever Yours*	

Bill Sparks Mysteries
  Murder in the Backcountry*

Nick McCord Mysteries
  Vol – 1 Murder at Gill's Point
  Vol – 2 Death of a Flower
  Vol – 3 A Dead Man's Treasure
  Vol – 4 Blackjack, A Game to Die For
  Vol – 5 Death on the Lakes
  Vol – 6 Secrets Can Get You Killed

Peter Blackstone Mysteries	Frank Tidsdale Mysteries
Murder in the Foothills	Death by Design
Murder on the Crystal Blue	Death by Assassination
Murder of My Love	
Murder in the Dark of Night	

*Also Available in Large Print Editions
  Non-Fiction: Two Brother Go to War

JAKE MURDOCK, BOUNTY HUNTER

by
J.E. Terrall

Printed in the United States of America
First Printing / 2019 – www.lulu.com

Cover: Front and back covers by author, J.E. Terrall

Book Layout /
Formatting: J.E. Terrall
              Custer, South Dakota

JAKE MURDOCK, BOUNTY HUNTER

To
Harold F. Rossman, my father-in-law,
in honor of his love of
western stories

CHAPTER ONE

In the Beginning

Frank Murdock swung the heavy ax he was using to cut large chunks of wood into small enough pieces to fit in the wood burning stove. He already had stacked several cords of wood close to a small cabin in preparation for the coming winter. The cabin was located just a few yards from the Cheyenne River.

The sudden sound of horses on the hard ground caught Frank's attention. He knew Jake could not have gone to town and returned in such a short time. He stopped cutting wood and looked up to see three men coming toward their cabin. Frank set his ax down next to the chopping block and began walking out to greet the three riders as they rode toward the cabin.

The three men looked like they had been riding a long way. Frank also noticed they were well armed. Noticing the little things that could cause him harm was something he had learned when he was a policeman in Richmond, Virginia, before the Civil War.

"We got company, Millie," Frank called out while he watched the three riders approach the cabin.

Millie wiped her hands on her apron as she stepped to the door of the cabin and watched the riders as Frank walked toward them. She didn't recognize any of the men. It was clear to her that they were not from around there.

"Howdy," Frank said. "You look like you've come a long way. There's water in the trough for your horses. Where are you headed?"

"No place special. We was thinkin' 'bout goin' ta Deadwood for a spell," the older of the three said. "I hear there's still plenty of gold there."

"Well, you're headed in the right direction. I'm Frank Murdock, and that's my wife, Millie."

"Howdy, Ma'am," the older man said. "I'm Wilber Simon, and these are my two sons, Isaac and Noah."

"Good Christian names," Millie said with a smile.

"Yes, Ma'am. Good Christian names," Wilber said as he looked at Millie.

Frank noticed the two younger men were looking around as if they were looking for something. He got the impression they were looking to see if there was anyone else around. He also noticed Wilber was looking Millie over. Frank didn't like the way Wilber looked at his wife. He got the feeling they were not good people. Frank slowly started to move closer to his rifle which was leaning against a stack of cut wood only a few feet away.

Suddenly, there was the sound of a gun going off and Frank fell to the ground. Millie called out his name and ran to him. She knelt down and lifted Frank's head into her lap. He had difficulty breathing as he looked up at her. The look of fear came over his face just before he died in her arms.

Millie looked up to see the three men getting off their horses. The older man started walking toward her. She let go of Frank, stood up, then turned and ran as fast as she could toward the cabin. She just made it to the door when she felt a big hand grab her and swing her around. She fell on the porch of the cabin then turned and looked up at the older man.

Wilbur reached down, picked her up and forced her into the cabin. He threw her on the bed, ripped off her clothes and had his way with her. After he was finished, his two sons had their way with her before Isaac, the youngest, cut her throat and left her on the bed. When they were done, they took what food they wanted, and the two work horses that were in the corral, then rode off.

Quiet returned to the small ranch on the prairie. There was a light covering of snow on the ground where the sun couldn't reach it. A light breeze was coming out of the south bringing with it unusually warm weather for late October on the plains of the Dakota Territory in 1881.

In a corral, next to the barn where the two large work horses had been enjoying the bright sunshine and the warm weather, but were now gone. The only things in the corral were a couple of chickens scratching at the ground looking for grubs they hoped to find around the small barn and along the wooden corral.

Jake Murdock, their eighteen-year-old son, had left early that morning to take advantage of the unusually warm weather and sunny day to ride into town. His mother had ordered some material for a new dress, and she wanted him to go into town to pick it up for her. It would take him most of the day to go to town, get what his mother had ordered and return.

He also wanted to visit a girl he had met at a Fourth of July picnic held in the town a few months ago. He had not seen her since because of the work on his father's small ranch.

Jake had a little more education than the average young man in the area. His mother had been a teacher back in Virginia and had taught him to read and write, as well as some math. He had also learned to track and hunt from his father and from an Indian who had befriended his father when they first settled there.

Jake was tall, good looking and very strong. He had learned to use a rifle and pistol when he was very young. His father had taught him not to shoot unless he was sure he could hit what he aimed at, and to use a gun only when necessary. He spent many hours out behind the barn secretly practicing drawing and shooting his pistol when his father was busy, or while he was out watching over his father's small herd of cattle. As a result, he had become very fast with a pistol, as well as very accurate.

It was several hours after the three men had left the ranch with the two work horses, when Jake returned from town. When he was still some distance from the cabin, he thought he could see someone lying on the ground near the stack of wood. He kicked his horse in the sides and raced toward the cabin. Jake drew up next to his father and jumped off his horse and ran to him.

Jake quickly discovered his father was dead on the cold ground with a bullet hole in his chest. The first thing that came to his mind was where was his mother? Jake looked around but didn't see her. He noticed there were tracks from several sets of boots, including one that had some kind of plate nailed on the heel of the left boot. The tracks led toward the cabin. The cabin door was wide open.

Fearing the worst had happened, Jake ran to the cabin and looked inside. He saw his mother lying naked on the bed, and she was covered in blood. He quickly turned away, leaned up against the door frame and began to cry.

It took Jake several minutes to get his emotions under control. As soon as he could begin to think clearly, he knew what he had to do. Jake went to where his father lay, picked him up and carried him into the cabin. He laid his father on the bed next to his mother and covered them with a quilt his mother had made.

Jake realized there was no time to waste if he was going to get revenge for the murder of his parents, and revenge was what he wanted. He stepped out of the cabin and saw his horse had wandered over to the corral.

Jake walked over to his horse then tied it to the top rail of the corral. He took the cloth he had gotten for his mother off his saddle, then took it to the cabin where he spread it over his parents. He then gathered all the supplies he would need and carried them out to the corral. He packed the supplies in his saddlebags and tied a bedroll to his saddle.

As soon as Jake had everything he needed on his horse, and his horse was ready to travel, he went into the barn and found the can of coal oil his father kept to use in the lanterns. He took it to the cabin and splashed some of it around inside the cabin, the rest he splashed over the front of the cabin then tossed the can inside.

He stepped back and looked at the cabin he had helped his father build. After saying a short prayer his mother had taught him as a child, he then vowed to find and kill the men who had murdered his parents.

After he had done all he could, he took a match, lit it and set the cabin on fire. Jake stood in front of the cabin and watched as the flames quickly spread engulfing the entire cabin. The heat from the flames soon matched the heated anger he felt in his heart.

After making sure the cabin was burning well, he went to his horse, untied it and swung into the saddle. He looked back over his shoulder and watched the cabin burn for a few minutes more. When the roof began to fall in, he turned his horse and began following the tracks left by the five horses. He never looked back.

The two work horses that had been stolen now belonged to him. His hope was that the horses would help him find the men who had killed his parents. Their hoof prints would be much larger than the saddle horses that had come into the yard, and would leave a deep hoof print in the ground.

Since there were no roads that passed close to the Murdock ranch, Jake had to follow the trail left by the three men as they rode across the open prairie. The tracks were not hard to follow since one of the work horses left a distinctive imprint in the hard soil. The horse kicked up a bit of dirt with each step it took. The trail tended to head in a westerly direction toward the Black Hills.

As time passed, Jake kept an eye on the sky while making sure he didn't lose the tracks. There hadn't been any rain for a long time making it easy to follow the men. But almost any kind of a rain could easily wipe out their tracks making it almost impossible to find the three men.

Jake followed the tracks until it was almost too dark to see them. He drew up and looked around. He could see some big cottonwood trees off to the southwest, only a short distance off the trail he had been following. Knowing that where there were cottonwood trees on the prairie often meant there was water. He turned his horse and rode toward the cottonwood trees.

When he got to the trees, he discovered there was a shallow stream flowing in a southerly direction. He took a minute to look up and down the stream. He didn't see anything that might cause him harm, so he stepped out of the saddle. He took his rifle from the saddle scabbard and his bedroll off the saddle, then took the saddle off his horse. He led the horse to the stream to drink. When the horse had drunk its fill, he hobbled the horse so it could graze on the lush grass along the edge of the stream.

Jake rolled out his bedroll under a big cottonwood tree, laid his rifle on the bedroll then went about finding sticks of wood for a fire. As soon as he had a fire going, he fixed his supper then sat with his back against the tree to eat. When he finished eating, he scooted down on his bedroll, tucked his rifle up close to his side then pulled his blanket over him. He laid there looking into the fire and thinking about what had happened during the day. Jake again renewed his vow to find the three men who had killed his father and mother, and when he did, he would kill them. He would find them if it took the rest of his life.

He laid on the bedroll and watched the fire. When it had burned down to coals he dozed off to sleep. It was a restless sleep because he had much on his mind.

Just as the sun was starting to rise up over the horizon, Jake sat up and looked around. The first thing he saw was his horse standing in the green grass along the edge of the stream. The horse was looking off toward the east. Jake turned and looked toward the east. He saw two Indians coming toward him on their Indian ponies.

At first, Jake didn't recognize them. He picked up his rifle and prepared himself for a fight. It wasn't until they came closer that Jake realized they were friends. Jake stood up and waited for them to approach.

Gray Hawk was a Sioux warrior who had befriended Jake's father when he first built his ranch on the plains of the Dakota Territory in 1869. He was a strong, muscular Indian who knew well what it took to live on the open plains. Gray Hawk had taught Jake how to live and hunt on the plains, and how to track.

The other Indian was Walks Swiftly, Gray Hawk's son, and Jake's best friend. They had spent a lot of time growing up together and learning each other's ways. Over the years they had grown to be like brothers. They had camped, hunted, and fished together.

Jake raised his hand in greeting when Gary Hawk rode up. Both Gary Hawk and Walks Swiftly slid off their horses and gave Jake a greeting.

"We have followed you. We saw the tracks at your home," Gray Hawk said with a serious look on his face. "We have good idea what happened there. Did you set fire to your cabin?"

"Yes. They killed my father and mother. I put my father with my mother in the cabin so their spirits would be together always, then set the cabin on fire. I did not have time to bury them."

"You are going after the men?" Walks Swiftly asked, his voice showing his concern for his friend.

"Yes. I have to," Jake said. "I cannot let them get away with what they have done."

"We will go with you," Gray Hawk said.

"No. This is something I must do alone."

"But there were three of them. I saw their tracks in the ground, and the tracks of your father's work horses," Walks Swiftly said concerned for Jake because of the task he was taking on.

"I know, but they must know who it was they killed and know who is going to kill them. I will let them know before they die."

Gray Hawk didn't say anything more. He understood about revenge. He also knew what it could do to a man who killed another out of revenge or anger.

"We will be on our way. You have much to do," Gray Hawk said knowing that to say anything more would be a waste of time and effort.

Walks Swiftly looked at his father as if he should say something or do something. But when his father gave him a stern look, he got on his horse.

Jake watched as his friends rode away. As soon as they were out of sight, Jake fixed himself breakfast, put out his fire then saddled his horse. He took a quick look in the direction his friends had taken. He knew they had meant well, but this was something he had to do alone. He wondered if he would ever see his friends again. Not knowing what the future held, he mounted his horse and rode back to where he had left the trail of the three killers.

Once on their trail, he rode at a steady gait, one that would cover a lot of ground but would not tire his horse too quickly. Every so often he would stop, get down from his saddle to check the tracks made by the three riders and his work horses, then walk his horse for a little while before getting back in the saddle. It was around noon when he noticed the horses had slowed down to a slow walk. He stopped and got down to check the tracks again. He noticed one of the saddle horses had developed a limp causing it to leave a distinctive hoof print.

He looked across the open prairie as he thought about what might lie ahead. Jake remembered there was a small settlement on the Belle Fourche River just a few miles ahead. It wasn't much of a settlement as he recalled. There was only a blacksmith shop and livery stable, a trading post, and a saloon. The tracks seemed to be headed in that general direction. He thought the men he was tracking might go there and possibly try to trade the injured horse for a fresh one. It was the only place Jake could think where they might get a fresh horse or get the one limping treated for its injury.

As Jake got back on his horse, he looked up at the sky and noticed the clouds were starting to build off to the northwest. If it rained, he might lose their tracks. Hoping to get close enough to those he was tracking to see them before he lost their tracks, he began to push his horse a little harder toward the settlement.

As the day went on, the clouds grew thicker and darker. The settlement on the Belle Fourche River came into view just as the clouds opened up and it started to rain. Jake got off his horse, unpacked his slicker and put it on. He then got back in the saddle and pressed on toward the settlement.

By the time he got to the settlement, it was raining fairly hard. He rode up to the livery stable. The door was open and there was a short stocky man leaning against the door watching it rain.

"Come on in. Ain't no sense in standin' out there in the rain."

Jake rode into the stable then stepped out of the saddle.

"You can put your horse in the stall over there," the owner said as he pointed to an empty stall.

Jake nodded, then led his horse to the stall the man had pointed to, then took off the saddle.

"How much to stable my horse here?" Jake asked.

"Two bits for the night, two bits for feed, and two bits if I have to rub him down for ya."

Jake smiled, then reached into his pocket and took out four bits. He handed it to the man.

"I'll rub him down. He doesn't take kindly to strangers."

"He ain't mean, is he?" the owner said with a concerned look on his face.

"No, he just doesn't like strangers touching him. He won't give you any trouble if you don't touch him when I'm not around."

Jake looked at the other horses in the barn. He immediately recognized the two work horses in the stalls directly across from the one he put his horse in. They were the horses stolen from his father's place.

"Who owns those two work horses?" Jake asked.

Jake turned and looked at the owner of the livery stable while taking off his slicker. He hung his slicker up on a nail sticking out of the post at the corner of the stall.

"Funny you should ask. I just bought them from three men who came in here about two hours ago. Are you interested in buying them?"

"No. I'm not interested in buying them since I already own them."

The look on the livery stable owner's face was priceless. He looked at Jake then at the horses.

"Where will I find the men who sold you the horses?" Jake asked.

While Jake waited for the livery stable owner to answer him, he removed the bridle from his horse then took a rag and rubbed the horse dry. When he finished, he stepped out of the stall.

The livery stable owner looked at Jake for a moment. He wasn't sure what was going on, but he knew that whatever it was, it wasn't going to be good.

"Say, what's your name, young fella?"

"Jake Murdock. The brand on those horses' right flank is 'FM', my father's initials. What's your name?"

"I'm Sam Albertson. I didn't know they was your horses. Three men came in here wanting to sell 'um. The guy said he was Franklin Miller and showed me the brand," he said looking at Jake and the gun he wore.

"I'm not mad at you. Those men killed my father and mother, and stole the horses. I intend to make them pay for that."

"What about the horses?"

"You paid for them, they're yours. I don't have a need for work horses. I'll collect the money from them," Jake said with a hint of confidence in his voice.

Sam watched Jake draw his gun from his holster and check it. After putting it back in the holster, he pulled his rifle from the saddle scabbard and checked it.

"Say, you ain't goin' up again them three alone, are you?"

"You got a better idea?" Jake asked. "I doubt you have any kind of lawman here."

"Well, no, we ain't," Sam admitted.

"I guess if I want justice, I'll have to get it myself."

"You sure it's justice you want?"

"Did they go to the saloon?" Jake asked ignoring Sam's question.

Jake knew he had little interest in justice, he wanted revenge and he was going to get it if it was the last thing he did.

"Yeah," Sam answered reluctantly.

Jake nodded his head. He turned and walked out of the livery stable with his rifle firmly in his left hand. It was still raining and the street had turned to mud, but Jake hardly noticed. He walked toward the saloon with only one thing on his mind, to kill the three man whose names he did not know nor wanted to know.

As Jake approached the saloon, he levered a round into the chamber and made sure the rifle was ready to shoot. Holding the rifle in his left hand, he held it with his finger on the trigger. He reached for his pistol with his right hand, then lifted it up and set it back loosely in his holster, making sure he would be able to draw it quickly and smoothly.

As he stepped up on the boardwalk in front of the saloon, he moved up close to the window and peeked inside. There were five people in the saloon, the barkeeper behind the bar, an old man sitting in the corner nursing a beer, and three men at the bar.

One of the men at the bar was older than the other two. He was short, stocky and had a pot belly. He wore his gun high on his right hip and he was standing with his back to the bar, leaning against it. He held a beer in his right hand. The man had a clear view of anyone who would come into the saloon.

The other two were younger and looked like they might be the older man's sons. One of them was tall and wore his gun on his right side and tied down on his leg like he thought he was some kind of a gunfighter. The shorter one looked to be about Jake's age, but he was a little shorter than Jake and not as muscular. He wore his gun on his right hip like his father.

Jake studied the three of them for a couple of minutes. He was sizing them up. Trying to figure which one he would have to take first. He decided the taller young man was the biggest threat to his success. Next was the older man, then the kid.

Taking a deep breath, Jake readied himself then stepped up to the door. He pushed the door open, stepped inside then moved to the side so there was a wall at his back.

The older man looked at him while his two sons slowly turned around to see who had come in. They stood there for a second before anyone made a move. The older man must have thought he saw something in Jake's face, or thought he looked like his father. He let the glass of beer fall from his hand as he started for his gun. Jake quickly jerked his rifle up and fired one shot that hit the older man in the stomach, doubling him over.

The suddenness of what was happening caused the tall man to glance at his father causing him to hesitate just a second or two before reaching for his gun. His hesitation was time enough for Jake to draw his pistol and shoot the taller man in the chest. He collapsed on the floor, dead before he could even clear leather.

The kid froze, not sure what was going on. The sounds of gunshots, the smell of burnt gunpowder, and seeing his father and brother fall so quickly caused the kid to not make a move. He had not even reached for his gun. He just stood there looking at Jake with fear in his eyes.

Nothing was said by either of them for several seconds. Jake could see the kid's hands trembling.

"The three of you killed my parents. My name is Jake Murdock. You shot my father in cold blood, then raped and killed my mother," Jake said without a hint of anger in his voice. "I want you to know who is going to kill you."

The kid just stood there, not moving or saying anything.

"You have a choice," Jake said. "You can either draw that gun of yours, or you can drop your gun belt on the floor and be hung on that old cottonwood tree at the edge of town for murder and horse stealing."

Keeping a close eye on the kid, Jake slipped his pistol back into his holster.

The kid looked around the saloon as if he was hoping that someone would come to his aid. The barkeeper had moved down to the end of the bar away from the kid while the old man stood up and moved well out of the line of fire. Both the barkeeper and the old man watched the kid and wondered what he would do.

It was clear to the kid that no one was going to help him, and he really had no choice. His only chance to keep on living was to draw against the man who had just killed his father and brother.

Jake noticed the kid look down at the floor and take a deep breath. He knew the kid had decided what he had to do. He was working up the courage to draw against Jake. Jake had given the kid more of a chance than they had given his parents.

Suddenly, the kid grabbed for his gun. The end of the barrel had not cleared his holster when a bullet hit him square in the chest slamming him back against the bar. The kid looked up at Jake with a surprised look on his face, then he slumped forward and fell dead on the floor.

Jake stood near the door to the saloon and looked at what he had done. He had never killed a man before, but he felt no sorrow for the death of the men he had just killed. He looked at them as nothing more than wild animals who had killed his parents and needed to be killed.

He walked over to the men he had shot, then searched each one of them for the money they had from selling the horses they had stolen from his parent's small ranch. As he stood up and put the money in his pocket, he looked at the barkeeper who had been watching him. He felt the need to say something.

"This is the money they got from selling the horses they stole from my father after they killed him and my mother," he said.

The barkeeper simply nodded then watched Jake as he turned and started for the door. Jake stopped and turned around when the barkeeper spoke.

"What do I do with them?" the barkeeper asked.

"You can bury them in your cemetery, if you have one, or you can drag them out on the prairie and leave them to the coyotes and vultures. I don't care what you do with them," Jake said, then he turned and walked out of the saloon.

It was still raining when Jake walked out of the saloon and toward the livery stable, but he hardly noticed. When he got to the livery stable, the owner was standing just inside the door. Jake walked by him without saying a word. He walked toward the stall where he had left his horse.

"You ain't plannin' on leavin' in this weather, are ya?" Sam asked when Jake reached for the bridle for his horse.

Jake stopped and looked at Sam. He thought for a moment before saying anything.

"I doubt I'm very welcome here after what I just did. I should be moving on."

"I wouldn't worry too much about the folks that live here. You did what you had to do. They don't take kindly to murderers or horse thieves. You can stay here in the stable if you've a mind to. Ain't no one goin' to bother ya here."

Jake looked around the stable, then looked at Sam.

"Maybe I can sleep in the loft out of sight," Jake suggested.

"That would be fine. Have you had anything to eat?"

"Not since this morning," Jake admitted.

"I'll have the wife fix ya something. Why don't ya sit down for a spell?"

Jake looked at Sam for a moment before he nodded, then sat down on a bale of hay. He watched Sam leave the livery stable. It wasn't very long before Sam returned to the livery stable with a plate covered with a red and white checkered cloth napkin in one hand, and a mug of coffee in the other. Sam handed it to Jake then sat down on another bale of hay next to Jake.

"It ain't much, but it will fill your stomach," Sam said with a grin.

Jake uncovered it and found a large piece of meat, a baked potato, and a serving of corn bread. He immediately began eating. He ate without talking. Sam seemed to understand Jake not wanting to talk and let him eat in peace. The meal was good. As soon as he was finished, Jake gave the plate and mug to Sam.

"Thanks for the meal. Would you be so kind as to tell your wife thank you for me?"

"Sure thing. I've got a question for ya."

"What is it?"

"What do I do with the three horses belongin' to those three men?"

"You might as well keep them. They don't have any use for them, and I certainly don't have a use for them."

"I guess you're right about that," Sam said. "I guess I'll leave ya to get some rest. Will I see you in the morning?"

"I'll be on my way at sunup," Jake said. "Thanks for all you've done for me."

"You can stop back anytime. You'll be welcome here," Sam said, then left the livery stable.

Jake watched as Sam walked down the street. It wasn't long before he returned to the barn with the three horses. Sam unsaddled the horses, putting the saddles with their saddlebags and bedrolls over the top rail of one of the stalls. He then rubbed down the horses.

"I'll take care of the saddles and bags in the morning," Sam said.

"You can keep whatever you find in them. It might help pay for their keep."

"Thanks. Sleep well," Sam said then turned and headed for the house.

As soon as Sam was inside his house, Jake closed the barn door. He took his bedroll and climbed up into the loft. Jake rolled out his bedroll on the straw and laid down. He could hear the sound of the rain as it fell on the roof and the shuffling of the horses in the stalls below him. It was soothing for him.

Jake thought about what he had done as he laid there looking up at the ceiling. He cried softly for the death of his parents, but felt no remorse for the three men he had killed in the saloon. It wasn't long before he drifted off to sleep. It was the first good night's sleep he'd had since the night before he went to town for the cloth for his mother.

When morning came and the sun came up over the horizon, Jake was on his horse and riding west toward the Black Hills. He never once looked back.

CHAPTER TWO

Winter in Hill City

A week and a half after Jake killed the three men in the small village on the Belle Fourche River out on the prairie, he rode into the small mining town of Hill City in the Black Hills. The weather had turned cold and it looked like winter was finally coming to the hills. It crossed his mind he might want to find a place where he could stay for the winter. In order to do that, he would have to find a job.

Jake rode his dusty and dirty buckskin horse past the Baptist Church and down the street to the livery stable. He turned his horse toward the hitching rail, then sat in the saddle as he looked around. He turned his head back around when he heard the door to the livery stable open.

Standing in front of him was a stocky man with strong muscular arms. He was wearing a heavy leather apron over a shirt that had once been white, and dark colored pants. In his big grimy hands, he held a heavy hammer in one hand and tongs in the other. It was clear he was the local blacksmith and he had been working next to a fire.

"Somethin' I can do for ya?" the man asked.

"Yes. I'd like to stable my horse here for the night," Jake said.

"Sure. It'll be two bits for the night. If ya feed him my hay and oats, that'll be another two bits for the feed. He looks like he could use a good rubdown, I'll take care of that for another two bits."

"I'll pay for the night and the feed, but it would be best if I rub him down. He doesn't take kindly to strangers touching him unless I'm with him."

"He ain't mean, is he?" the blacksmith asked worried that the horse might cause damage to the stalls.

"No, he ain't mean. He just doesn't like strangers touching him. Once he gets used to you, he's as gentle as any horse you've ever seen," Jake said with a smile.

"I don't want no mean horse bustin' up my stalls."

"He won't do any damage to your stable," Jake assured the blacksmith.

"Okay. You can put him in the second stall on the left, but if he damages my stable, you'll have to pay for it."

"That's fair enough," Jake replied.

Jake got off his horse, reached into his pocket and pulled out four bits. After handing it to the blacksmith, he led his horse into the stall, filled a pail with water from the pump in front of the stable and gave it to his horse. He put some feed and hay in the trough in the front of the stall for the horse.

As soon as his horse was eating, Jake turned and saw the blacksmith watching him from the door. He walked up to the blacksmith and smiled.

"He'll be all right for now. I'll be back to rub him down when he's finished eating. Can you tell me where I can get something to eat?"

"Sure. You'll find the Hill City Café on the other side of the street right next to the assayer's office. It's about five or six buildings down. They got good food and plenty of it," the blacksmith said. "You can get somethin' to eat at most of the saloons, but the food's a lot better at the café."

"Thanks."

"Say, young man, what's your name. I think I've seen you 'afore."

"The name's Jake Murdock."

"Na. I thought ya was someone else. Are ya goin' to be around long?"

"That depends on if I can find a job. You know of anyone looking for help?"

"Yeah. Ya any good with a gun?"

"I do all right. Why?" Jake asked, curious why he would ask such a question.

"I heard the town marshal was looking for some help. I think he's lookin' for a deputy. We got lots of saloons here. He thinks he needs a little help. Like he says. 'I can't be two places at once'," the blacksmith said with a slight chuckle in his voice.

"I'll check it out. Thanks for the help."

Jake left the livery stable and crossed the street, then walked down the street to the Hill City Café. After getting a good meal, he stepped out on the boardwalk and looked up and down the street. When he saw the marshal's office, he turned and started walking toward it.

Just as he walked by one of the saloons, a man came out of it in a bit of a hurry. The man ran into Jake, almost knocking him off the boardwalk.

"Get the hell out of the way," the big man said sharply.

"Excuse me, but it seems you are the one who ran into me. You are the one who needs to watch where he is going," Jake said calmly as he straightened up.

"How'd you like your face smashed in?"

"Not very well, I would guess. Why? Are you thinking you want to try?" Jake said with a slight smile.

The big man turned slightly away from Jake, made a fist he thought Jake wouldn't see, then swung around quickly. Jake had seen him make a fist and was ready. He ducked the man's fist, then quickly planted his fist hard in the big man's gut causing the big man to double over. Jake then hit him hard on the back of the neck sending the big man crashing to the ground, face down.

The big man slowly rolled over and looked up at Jake with hate in his eyes. He started to reach for his gun, but he didn't clear leather before Jake kicked the big man in the face breaking his nose.

With his hand over his broken nose, the big man looked up at Jake. From the look in the big man's eyes, he knew he had been beaten.

"We can end this right now and walk away, or you can press your luck," Jake said. "I don't want to have to kill you; but if you press it, I will."

"No. I've had enough," the big man said sounding defeated.

Jake reached out a hand to the big man and said, "Let me help you up. I'll help you to the doctor's office."

The big man looked up at Jake's hand then at his face for a moment. He slowly reached up and took Jake's hand, not sure if it was some kind of trick. Jake grabbed his hand and helped him up then walked with him to the doctor's office. As soon as the doctor started treating the big man, Jake left and headed over to the marshal's office.

When he stepped inside the marshal's office, Jake found the town marshal sitting in his chair next to the window. The marshal smiled at Jake then motioned toward a chair.

"Have a seat. I'm Marshal John Walker. That was quite some display you put on across the street."

"I'm sorry about that. My name's Jake Murdock."

"You handled Big Mike pretty well. I don't think you will have any more trouble from him."

"I hope not."

"What is it I can do for you?"

"Well, sir. I'm looking for a job. The blacksmith said you might be looking for a deputy."

"Have you got any experience as a deputy?"

"No, sir."

"Have you ever shot a man?" the marshal asked looking at Jake as if he was a little young to have killed anyone.

"Yes, sir," Jake said softly.

"Oh. When was that?"

"About a week and a half ago."

"You want to tell me about it?"

"Not much to tell. Three men, a man and his two sons, killed my father then raped and murdered my mother. I hunted them down and caught up with them at a little settlement on the plains over east of here. I killed all three of them in the saloon."

"I heard word of three men headed this way after killing a store keeper over by Chamberlain. It was a man and his two sons. The man was Wilbur Simon, and his sons Isaac and Noah. Names ring a bell with you?"

"No, but it could have been them. I never asked them their names."

"The stagecoach driver told me about a young man who killed three men in a saloon, then left them for the town to bury. Was that you?"

"Might have been, I killed the three of them in a little saloon."

"The stagecoach driver said the barkeeper told him that he ain't never seen anyone so quick with a gun."

"Do you have a job for me, sir?" Jake asked politely, not wanting to talk about it.

"I sat here and watched the way you handled Big Mike. You could have shot him and no one would have blamed you, but you didn't. Why?"

"He didn't need killing. He was drunk and mad at someone. I just happened to be the first person he thought he could take his anger out on."

"Whatever the reason, you did a good thing out there. I seriously doubt you will have any trouble with him again."

"I'm still interested in finding out if you have a job for me," Jake said impatiently. He didn't really want to talk about the men he had killed.

"I'll put you on. It pays thirty dollars a month plus a room at Sharon's boarding house. You take your meals there, or you pay for them yourself if you don't eat there. Since you have a horse, it pays for boarding your horse at the livery stable. Feed is included, but all other care for your horse is up to you. You can take care of your horse or pay Joe to do it for you. Any questions?"

"Yes, sir. When do I start?"

"Right now. Raise you right hand and repeat after me."

Jake raised his right hand and recited the words the marshal said. When he was done, the marshal reached in the drawer of his desk, pulled out a deputy marshal's badge and handed it to Jake.

"You wear this badge whenever you're on duty. For the next week you will work with me. I will introduce you to the shop keepers and saloon owners and some of the madams around town. Try to get along with them, but don't take any guff from 'um. I'll do my best to teach you what you need to know. Try to avoid gunfights as much as you can, but protect yourself and any bystanders. Part of bein' a good marshal is using your head instead of your gun when you can, something like you did with Big Mike. But don't hesitate to use your gun if you feel you have to, okay?"

"Yes, sir."

"You don't need to call me, sir. You can call me, marshal or John. Take your things over to Sharon's boarding house and get settled in. I'll see you back here in the morning. We'll plan out the day then," John said.

"Yes, sir."

"John," the marshal reminded him.

"John," Jake said with a grin.

Jake left the marshal's office and walked back to the livery stable. He gave his horse a good rubdown, then settled him in for the night. When he was finished, he took his saddlebags and bedroll then went to Sharon's boarding house. Sharon showed him to the room he was to use. It was located in the front of the boarding house overlooking the main street. He put his things in his room then took a walk around the town in order to familiarize himself with the town and where different stores and saloons were located.

When he finished his stroll down Main Street, he had discovered that there was a church at each end of town with fifteen saloons and brothels between them. He stopped in a couple of the saloons to just look around on his way back to the boarding house. He learned from a couple of barkeepers that the ministers and some of the locals called the main street of Hill City between the two churches "One Mile of Hell".

Jake then returned to the boarding house where he had dinner. After dinner, he went to the livery stable and checked on his horse. He took a minute to thank the blacksmith for telling him that the marshal was looking for a deputy. He also learned the blacksmith's name was Joe Wilcox. Once he had his horse settled in for the night, he headed for the boarding house in the hope of getting a good night's sleep.

Since it had been a long day, Jake got ready for bed as soon as he got to his room. He laid down on the bed and thought about what it might be like to be a deputy marshal in a small mining town. It wasn't long and he drifted off to sleep.

Jake spent his first week on the job walking the streets of Hill City with the town marshal. He was introduced to almost all of the barkeepers, saloon owners and shop owners, as well as the madams who ran the brothels. He was even introduced to several of the young women who worked in the brothels. The marshal told Jake there were no rules that prevented him from visiting any of the young women who worked in the brothels as long as it didn't interfere with his duties as a lawman, and it was on his own time.

It wasn't long before Jake was making the rounds of the brothels and saloons by himself. During his rounds, he met a number of the working girls, but made it a point not to get too close to any of them. The working girls were often the cause of the fights between the men. He didn't want to appear to take sides when that happened.

Saturday nights, both Jake and John worked, but not often together. The miners got paid on Saturday and spent most, if not all, their money on gambling, liquor and women, frequently ending in fights. It seemed Jake was always arresting three or four, sometimes as many as eight or nine, miners for drunk and disorderly, or drunk and slapping one of the working girls round. There was also the occasional wild drunk miner who tried to shoot up a bar or get into a gunfight with another drunk.

Occasionally, a cowboy would come to town. For some reason that Jake could never understand, when a cowboy came to town, Jake often ended up breaking up a fight between the cowboy and a miner. They just didn't seem to get along.

On one Saturday night in late January, Jake walked by a saloon on his usual rounds of the town. He stopped and looked inside to make sure all was peaceful. He quickly discovered that there was an argument between a cowboy and one of the local miners. The miner was standing in the corner with a knife held at the neck of a pretty young working woman, while the cowboy stood next to the end of the bar with his gun pointed at the miner in the corner. At the moment, it looked like a standoff. The young woman looked like she was scared to death that the miner would kill her. The cowboy wanted the young woman, and the miner wasn't about to let him have her, both of them appeared to be drunk.

Jake looked at the situation and quickly realized what was going on and that he needed to put an end to it before someone got killed. As Jake stepped into the saloon, the cowboy quickly turned and pointed his gun at Jake.

"Hold on, fella," Jake said as he held his hands away from his gun. "You don't want to do something that will get you hung."

Jake's comment seemed to calm the cowboy a little. Although he still had his gun pointed at Jake, he appeared to be thinking. It was clear he wasn't so sure he was doing the right thing.

"Put the gun on the bar," Jake said quietly. "We don't want anyone getting hurt."

"What about him?" the cowboy asked. "He has to put his knife down."

"When you put your gun down, he will put his knife down."

The cowboy looked at Jake, then at the miner. He wasn't sure what he should do. After a moment, the cowboy reluctantly put his gun on the bar.

"I ain't lettin' him have this girl. She's mine," the miner insisted, his voice slurred due to too much alcohol.

"Listen to me. You need to let the girl go. You don't want to hurt her."

"I don't want him to have her. He'll hurt her."

"Let her go so she can come to me," Jake said. "I'll see to it she's safe."

The miner looked from the cowboy to Jake. He was trying to decide what he should do. It slowly sank into his alcohol soaked brain that he really didn't have a choice. The deputy was not going to let him keep the girl.

Jake glanced at the cowboy. He noticed the cowboy was looking at his gun. Jake casually moved a little closer to the cowboy.

Just as the miner took the knife away from the girl's throat and allowed the girl to move away, the cowboy reached for his gun. Jake was ready. He drew his gun and laid the barrel over the cowboy's head knocking him to the floor. The cowboy was out cold.

"Okay, this is over. You drop the knife or I'll put a hole in you," Jake said with a sharp tone of authority while pointing his gun at the miner.

The miner dropped the knife on the floor and stepped back away from it. Jake motioned for the miner to come over to the bar. The miner did as he was told.

"Pick him up," Jake said as he pointed at the cowboy.

"What? I ain't pickin' him up."

"You're picking him up, or you'll by laying right beside him."

"What am I supposed to do with him?" the miner asked looking a little confused.

"You're going to pick him up and carry him to the jail. If you drop him just once, you will have a knot on your head just like his. Now pick him up," Jake ordered.

Jake grabbed the cowboy's gun and stuck it in his belt, then watched as the miner picked up the cowboy. Jake followed them out the door and marched them down the street to the jail. When they arrived at the jail, he had the miner put the cowboy in one cell, then he locked up the miner in the other cell. After the miner was locked up, he locked the cell the cowboy was in just as he was coming around.

"Now both of you are going to sleep it off right where you are. If I have any trouble with either of you, I'll put you to sleep. You understand?"

"Yes, sir," the miner said softly.

"Yeah," the cowboy said as he touched the knot on the back of his head.

Once Jake had the two drunks taken care of, he returned to making his rounds. It didn't take long for the story of what had happened to get around. Whenever Jake walked into a saloon or brothel, everyone seemed to take notice, and it often got very quiet.

Jake made it a point to stop in at the saloon where he had the run-in with the miner and the cowboy. He stopped in to see how the girl was doing. It had to have been a frightening experience the young girl would not soon forget.

"Where's the young woman that the miner had his knife to her throat?" Jake asked the barkeeper.

"She was pretty shaken up and went to her room, alone."

"Where is her room?"

"Top of the stairs, third door on the left."

Jake nodded that he understood and went up the stairs. He walked down the hall and found her room. He knocked lightly on the door. It took a moment or so before she answered the door. She opened the door just far enough to see who was there. At first, she looked scared, but as soon as she saw who it was she smiled and opened the door so he could enter her room.

"Come in," she said.

As soon as Jake stepped inside the room, she shut the door.

"I stopped by to see how you are doing."

"I'm fine thanks to you."

"Good. What's your name?"

"Suzanna."

"It's nice to meet you, Suzanna. I'm Jake Murdock."

"Yes, I know. I've seen you stop in the saloon from time to time. I think you were making your rounds," she said with a smile.

"Yes. I just wanted to stop in and make sure you are all right. I'd better get back to work."

"Do you have to leave?" she said wishing he could stay longer.

"I have to finish making rounds and keep things quiet."

"When do you get off work?"

"It'll be about midnight or maybe a little later."

"Could you stop by for a cup of coffee when you're done?"

Jake looked at her. He didn't miss the fact that she was pretty. She was also about his age.

"I'd like that, but are you sure it won't be too late?"

"No. I'll be waiting for you," she said with a smile.

Jake looked at her for a moment then turned and opened the door. He stepped out of the room and turned back to look at her again.

"I'll try not to be too late," Jake said then turned and walked down the hall.

Jake was almost to the stairs that led to the bar when he heard the door close behind him. He smiled to himself as he walked down the stairs.

As Jake made his rounds of the town, he couldn't get a picture of Suzanna out of his mind. Her long blond hair, the smooth complexion of her skin and her very nice figure kept him thinking about her. He had not met very many women, and certainly not one as pretty as Suzanna.

It was almost one in the morning when Marshall Walker told Jake he could call it a night. Things quieted down and it didn't look like there would be any more problems for the rest of the night. Jake bid John goodnight, then walked down the street to the Silver Dollar Saloon and brothel.

When Jake entered the Silver Dollar Saloon, he found the saloon was empty except for the barkeeper who was sweeping the floor. The barkeeper turned to see who had come in.

"Can I help you, Deputy?"

"I'm here to see Suzanna."

"She's up in her room," the barkeeper said with a smile.

Jake nodded that he understood and went up the stairs. He walked down the hall and knocked on the third door on the left. While he waited for a response, he looked up and down the hall. The hall was empty and the place was quiet.

When he heard the door latch, he turned around. The door opened slowly. He could see Suzanna peek around the edge of the door. As soon as she saw who was there, she opened the door.

"Hi," she said as she smiled at him.

"Is it too late for me to visit you?" Jake asked.

"No," she said as she opened the door wide enough for him to enter. She stepped back so he could enter the room.

Jake took off his hat as he stepped into the room and closed the door behind him. He looked at Suzanna and liked what he saw. She was wearing a thin satin robe opened to her waist. Under it she was wearing a silk, lacy night gown. He had not missed the fact she had a very nice figure and a beautiful face.

"Would you like to sit down?" she asked, the look in her eyes telling him that she hoped he would.

Jake didn't answer her, he simply walked across the room to a settee and sat down. He watched her every step as she walked toward him. She stopped in front of him.

"I'm glad you came by. I've been wanting to meet you," she said.

"You have?" he asked.

"Yes."

"I've seen you several times while making my rounds. I've been wanting to meet you, too."

"Why didn't you say something to me?" she said as she sat down beside him on the settee."

"You're so beautiful and I'm just a plain sort of man," he said shyly.

"I think you're very handsome," she said.

"You do?"

"Yes," she said with a smile as she reached out and put her hand over his.

Jake and Suzanna spent the next couple of hours talking in an effort to get to know each other. It wasn't long before Suzanna leaned over and kissed Jake. He liked the kiss even though he was a little surprised that she had kissed him. It wasn't long before Jake ended up in her bed, then spent the rest of the night in her arms.

Jake spent the rest of the winter in Hill City working as a deputy. Many a night was spent with Suzanna. They shared some of their past with each other. Jake found it easy to talk to her about almost anything. They eventually began talking about leaving Hill City and finding a place to start a ranch and raise a family.

Jake needed money to buy the land and get a few head of cattle in order to make their dreams become a reality. The opportunity came one day in the spring, an opportunity to get at least some of the money they would need.

CHAPTER THREE

Jake becomes a Bounty Hunter

On an early spring day in 1882 Jake walked out of the Silver Dollar Saloon and down the street to the marshal's office after another night with Suzanna. As he walked in the door, he saw Marshal Walker thumbing through some papers that had come in on yesterday's stagecoach. Marshal Walker looked up.

"Good mornin' Jake."

"Mornin' John. What do you have there?"

"It's a bunch of wanted posters. They came in on the afternoon stage. Yesterday's."

"Anyone wanted from around here?"

"Just one. He's wanted by the Custer County Sheriff."

"What for?"

"It seems he shot and killed the freight station manager while robbing the freight station. In his effort to escape, he ran over a woman with his horse. Apparently, one of the horses' hooves hit the woman in the head. She died a short time later in the doctor's office. Her young son was crossing the street with her. She managed to push him out of the way before the horse ran over her. The young boy was not injured."

"That wanted poster didn't give you all that information. How do you know it happened that way?" Jake asked.

"There was an additional information sheet added to the back of the poster that tells what happened."

The fact a woman was killed in front of her young son caused Jake to grow angry. Although Jake had not seen his mother and father killed, he knew all too well how it had affected him. Jake was sure the boy would carry the sight of his mother's death for the rest of his life. He turned red as anger grew within him.

"Are you all right? You need some time off?" John asked noticing that Jake looked very angry.

"Maybe," he said.

Jake was deep in thought. John wasn't sure that Jake had heard his question.

"What's on your mind, Jake?"

"Is there a description of the robber or about his horse or anything that would help find this guy?"

"It says here on the poster they think he is the same guy who robbed a freight station in the Wyoming Territory, just across the territorial line. He killed a man there, too. There's no description except that he was tall with dark brown hair. It seems the witnesses couldn't agree on anything."

"How much is the reward for catching him?"

"You thinking about going after him?" John asked, a hint of concern in his voice.

"I might. It's one way to get enough money to help me buy a ranch for Suzanna and me."

"True, but it ain't easy being a bounty hunter."

"I know how to track and how to handle a gun. I know what it takes to find a killer. I've done it."

"That you have. That you have," John said looking at Jake for a moment. "Okay. The reward is five hundred dollars, dead or alive."

"I think I'd like to take some time off."

"How much time?"

"A couple of weeks, maybe a month."

The marshal looked at Jake for a minute while he thought about Jake and what he was planning to do. He had grown close to Jake and liked him, but was reluctant to give him the time off. He thought about it for a minute before he decided what he would do.

"Okay. I'll hold your job open for you for one month. If you're not back by then I'll be looking for a new man. You understand?"

"Yes, sir."

"It's still John. Now all you have to do is tell Suzanna. I doubt she will like the idea very much."

Jake looked at John. His comment about having to tell Suzanna caused Jake to think about it. He was sure she would not like him going off to hunt a man, especially a man who had killed several people. Jake nodded his head, then turned and walked out the door. He walked down the street to the Silver Dollar Saloon.

Jake was deep in thought when he walked into the Silver Dollar Saloon. As he walked toward the stairs, he glanced over at the bar and gave a half-hearted wave to the barkeeper who was behind the bar washing glasses. The barkeeper simply nodded his head to acknowledge Jake's greeting.

He continued up the stairs, then down the hall to Suzanna's room. Jake knocked lightly on the door. He heard Suzanna tell him to come in.

"I saw you coming this way. I thought you went to work," she said, surprised that he had returned so soon.

"I did, but I've decided to take some time off."

"Oh," she said with a smile. "What are you planning?"

"I'm going to leave for a little while? I don't think I'll be gone for more than a month."

"A month!" Suzanna said sharply. "Where are you going?"

"I'm going to Custer City, but I don't know where it will take me from there."

"Why there?"

He hesitated for a moment before answering her. He thought about telling her some story about why he was leaving her for a month, but he couldn't lie to her.

"I'm hoping to find the man who killed several people including a woman in Custer City. I hope to at least find out where he might have gone. If it works out, we will have enough money to start looking for a ranch."

"You're going to hunt a killer?" she asked with a bit of sharpness in her voice.

"Yes."

"Since there is money involved, does that mean you are going to be a bounty hunter?"

Jake thought for a moment before he answered her.

"Yes. I guess it does. It is not the first time I have hunted a killer," he said.

"I wish you wouldn't go," Suzanna said as she stepped up to him and put her hands on his shoulders and looked into his eyes.

"I don't want to go, but I will never make enough money as a deputy to save up enough for us to get a ranch," Jake said as he put his hands on her waist and looked into her eyes.

"What about mining? You could make some money that way, and you could do it on your time off."

"I would still have to spend time away from you. Most of the area around here is already claimed, and there's no telling how long it would take to make any money panning for gold."

Suzanna let out a sigh as she realized that he had made up his mind, and she would not be able to change it.

"When do you plan to leave?" she asked.

"I'll be leaving first thing in the morning."

"Can we spend today together?" she asked, still hoping that she might be able to change his mind.

"I have a few things to do before I go. They shouldn't take much time, then we can spend the rest of the day together."

"Okay. I'll wait here for you."

Jake kissed Suzanna then left her room. He first went over to the livery stable and talked to the blacksmith. The blacksmith checked Jake's horse's shoes then put new shoes on the horse. Jake brushed his horse and made sure he had plenty to eat, as well as to make sure he didn't give the blacksmith a hard time.

As soon as his horse was taken care of, Jake went over to the General Store where he bought what supplies he thought he would need. He bought extra cartridges for both his rifle and pistol, plus some food and a tarp for a shelter in case the weather turned bad and he had to sleep out in the open.

Once Jake was ready, he returned to the Silver Dollar Saloon where he spent the rest of the day with Suzanna. They spent a good part of the day in her bed. When evening came, they went to the Hill City Café for dinner then returned to Suzanna's room where they spent the night together.

When Jake woke in the arms of Suzanna, it was still dark. He wanted to get going. It had already been a week since the woman had been killed. It would be hard to find out where the killer had gone. The longer he put off going, the harder it would be to find the killer.

Jake rolled over and swung his legs over the side of the bed. He looked over his shoulder and found Suzanna looking at him. She looked so pretty lying in the bed. Just looking at her made it hard for Jake to leave.

"Do you have to leave?" Suzanna asked, hoping he would change his mind.

"Yes."

"I wish you wouldn't go. You could stay here and we could be together."

"I would like to stay here with you, but there's no future for us here. We would have nothing more than what we have right now. I want more for us. I want a place where we can raise a family and live the way we want."

Suzanna looked at him. It was obvious that she was disappointed and would miss him, but she could also understand why he was doing it. It was for a future away from the saloons for both of them, and away from the dangers of being a deputy for Jake.

It seemed there was nothing else for them to say. Jake got dressed then strapped on his gun. He then leaned over the bed and kissed Suzanna. He straightened up, told her he loved her then looked at her for a second before he turned and walked out the door.

Once he was outside her room, he stopped. He could hear her crying. He turned back around and reached for the doorknob, but stopped. Jake knew that if he went back into her room, he would not leave her. His desire to build a life for them was greater than his desire to stay with her now. He turned, went down the stairs and out the door. Jake walked into the livery stable and saddled his horse.

As soon as he was ready, he swung into the saddle and started down the street toward the end of town. When he came to the Silver Dollar Saloon, he looked up at the window of Suzanna's room. He saw her standing in the window watching him as he rode by. He smiled, winked at her and waved as he passed by the front of the saloon. She waved back at him then watched him until he was out of sight.

It was late-afternoon when Jake rode into the small town of Custer City, in the southern Black Hills. He stopped in front of the sheriff's office, then looked around. The street was quiet. There were only a few people on the wide dirt street. A large freight wagon with four teams of large oxen was turning around in the middle of the main street. A small boy stood on the boardwalk and watched as the big freight wagon slowly turned around. There were only a few horses on the street, all of them stood in front of the Gold Pan Saloon.

Jake stepped out of the saddle and tied his horse to the hitching rail in front of the sheriff's office. He stepped up on the boardwalk then went into the sheriff's office. He found the sheriff sitting at his desk.

"Good afternoon, sheriff. I'm Jake Murdock," he said as he stuck out his hand.

"I'm Sheriff Metcalf," he said as he stood up and reached out to shake Jake's hand. "What can I do for you, Deputy Murdock?"

"How did you know I was a deputy?"

"News travels fast in this part of the country. You work for Marshal Walker."

"I see. Well, I'm not here as a deputy. I'm here to find out what information you can provide on the man who killed the manager of the freight station and killed the woman he ran down with his horse in your town."

"What's your interest in him?"

"I want to find him and make him pay for what he has done."

"So, you're interested in the reward?" the sheriff said with a slight grin.

"Yes, I guess you could say that, but I'm also interested in putting an end to his killing. He has no respect for life, anyone's life."

"There's not much I can tell you about him. I have no idea who he is, what his name is, or where he might be from, or where he might be now."

"Is there anything you can add to the description of him, besides what's on the wanted poster?" Jake asked hoping there was something that would make it easier for him to identify the man if he found him.

"I don't know how much good it will do ya, but he rode a chestnut brown horse with three white stocking feet and a white diamond shaped blaze on its face. At least that's what the few witnesses could agree on."

"That might help. What about the man?"

"The kid told us he had a shiny gun, but no one else who saw him could remember a shiny gun. Most of us think it might have been the sun shining off his gun barrel. It was pretty bright that day. It seems about all anybody saw clearly was the shotgun he carried."

"I can understand that. Was it possible the kid saw one of those fancy nickel-plated guns?"

"I guess it's possible, but we haven't been able to confirm it," Sheriff Metcalf said after giving it some thought. "I certainly don't remember seeing anyone around these parts who has one. That's a pretty expensive gun."

"Yes, it is. Do you have any idea where he went from here?"

"No. It took a little while to get a posse together, but we did it in about fifteen minutes. We tracked him west toward the Wyoming border, but he turned north into Hell Canyon where we lost his trail. Oh, he went around Four Mile Stage Stop instead of riding past it on the road. He was probably worried about someone seeing him since he robbed a stage just a mile from there a couple of days before he robbed the freight station."

"Any thoughts on where he might have gone?"

"Not really, but I think he might have himself a place to hide somewhere around Hell Canyon. Maybe up in one of them box canyons or in a draw back up in there. It's pretty rough country back in there. That's just a guess, mind you."

"What makes you think that?" Jake asked.

"Like I said, it's just a guess, that, and the fact he has hit several places around here. Nothing very far from the canyon. That's also where we lost his trail."

"What places?"

"He hit a stagecoach about a mile west of Four Mile Stage Stop, hit a stagecoach between here and Hot Springs, he hit the freight station over near the Wyoming border, and of course, he hit the freight station here. He's killed three people, so far, counting the woman."

"I think it might be a good idea if I start my search for him around some of those canyons north of the road west of here, starting with Hell Canyon," Jake said thinking out loud.

"You plannin' on goin' it alone? That's pretty rough country back in there."

"I think it's best if I go alone. If I go with several men, he might get the idea we're looking for him. If I go alone, he might be easier to find, and he might not think too much about one man back in the canyon. He might think I'm just hunting. I'll do my best to make him think that."

"You might be right. Sounds like a good plan."

"Do you know if this guy acts alone?"

"As far as we can tell. No one has seen him with anyone, or seen anyone who might be covering his back or his escape."

"Any idea how he gets his information on what the freighters or stagecoaches are carrying?"

"No, but he seems to know. He might have someone working with him. He hasn't hit a single freighter, or stagecoach, that didn't have valuable freight."

"Thanks for the information. I would appreciate it if you don't tell anyone about our conversation, or that I am looking for him, just in case he has a friend or two here in town. It might be best if you say nothing at all about me."

"I understand. I won't say anything to anybody," Sheriff Metcalf said.

"Thanks, Sheriff," Jake said then shook hands with the sheriff before leaving his office.

Jake stepped off the boardwalk in front of the sheriff's office and untied his horse. Since it was late afternoon, he decided to head on out of town. He didn't want the word to get out that he was in the area. The longer he stayed in town, the greater the chance he would be recognized by someone who knew he had been a deputy marshal in Hill City.

Jake left town following the road west for several miles. It was one of the roads used by the stagecoach between Newcastle and Custer City. He kept an eye out for anyone who might be following him, but he didn't see anyone.

After he rode along the road for several miles, he came around a fairly sharp curve. He was unable to see anyone following him so he rode off the road and in among the trees. Using a deer trail in the woods, he moved among the trees and on up in among some rocks. He found a place where he could easily conceal his horse from anyone who might be using the road, and where he could settle in for the night. He took the saddle off his horse and hobbled him where there was grass enough to feed him. After taking care of his horse, he made camp. Jake built a small fire to cook his dinner over, then settled in after he finished eating. He let his fire burn down to a few coals then finally let it go out completely.

Once the fire was out and darkness had covered the land, he moved his bedroll away from where his fire had been then laid out his bedroll again. He sat down on the bedroll and leaned back against a boulder with his rifle laid across his lap and his pistol lying beside him in easy reach. With his horse close by to warn him of anyone or anything approaching him, he drifted off to sleep.

When morning came, Jake was up before daybreak. He fixed himself breakfast, then saddled his horse. Jake put out the fire, then stepped into the saddle. He began to move slowly through the woods heading west toward Hell Canyon. He had no desire to have anyone see him. He spent the better part of the day working his way along the edge of the woods while staying in the cover of the forest. He continued to watch for any tracks that had been made by shod horses.

It wasn't until he was close to the edge of Hell Canyon that he found tracks by a shod horse. The horse had traveled north near the edge of the canyon. Jake had never seen the tracks made by the man who robbed the freight stations. He had no idea if they were the tracks he had been trying to find. The fact he had been told by the sheriff the tracks of the killer's horse had headed north into Hell Canyon, and they were the only tracks he had seen, led him to think he might have found the tracks he had been hoping to find.

Since they were the only tracks made by a shod horse, he decided he would follow them. He rode off well to the side of the tracks so he wouldn't leave his tracks where they would be easy for someone else to see, yet, close enough to the tracks that he could still see the tracks he wanted to follow. He slowly followed the tracks for that day and most of the next day.

It was getting late on the second day of following the tracks. The sun would soon be setting over the ridge of the canyon to the west. It would not be long before he would not be able to follow the tracks due to darkness. Jake turned away from the tracks and rode up to a rocky outcropping some distance from the tracks. He wanted it to look like he was not following the tracks he had found should someone discover his tracks and be following him.

Once he was in among the rocks, he found a small patch of good thick grass and a small pool of water from a spring where his horse could graze and drink. After checking out the place for any signs of other riders in the area, he stepped out of the saddle, hobbled his horse, removed his saddle from his horse then began setting up camp for the night.

Jake had found a place where he could put up a shelter in front of a rocky cliff. He could see out over the clearing where his horse was grazing. It would also be easy for him to build a small fire without it being seen by anyone, unless they were very close.

Once he had finished setting up his camp, he built a small almost smokeless fire and fixed his dinner. When he finished eating, he put a pot of coffee on the fire then leaned back against the tree to wait until it was ready to drink. While he waited, he watched his horse graze.

Suddenly, his horse raised its head and looked off toward the north. Jake grabbed his gun and quickly rolled off to the side behind a tree. He laid at the base of the tree pointing his gun in the direction his horse was looking.

"Who goes there?" Jake called out but didn't get an answer.

Jake laid quietly on the ground as he scanned the area for any kind of movement. He also listened for any sound that would give him some idea who or what was out there and where they might be. He saw and heard nothing for several minutes. He was beginning to think it might have been a deer or some other animal moving in the forest, but he still didn't move.

The sound of a twig snapping drew his attention off to his left. Jake quickly turned his attention in that direction.

"You think that coffee might be ready to drink?" a voice from the forest asked.

"It might be if you make yourself known," Jake replied.

"I would appreciate it if you would not shoot me when I step out into the light of your fire."

"I will not shoot if you step out with your hands where I can see 'um."

Jake waited and watched. It was only a few seconds before he saw a man step into the light of his fire in the clearing. The man had his hands out away from his sides where Jake could see them.

The man was rather tall and dressed in jeans, a buckskin shirt and a wide brimmed hat. His boots were worn, but still in pretty good shape. Jake immediately noticed the rather large knife in his belt and a pistol slung low in a holster that was tied down on his right side. He carried a lever action rifle which he held loosely in his left hand. His left hand was on the forward grip of the rifle leaving his right hand free.

Jake may have been young, but he was no fool. He was attentive to every little detail no matter how unimportant it might seem; a practice he had learned from his father, and one that could save his life. The fact that the man didn't seem to have a horse nearby also caused Jake to use extreme caution.

There was nothing close to the rocky outcroppings except a few narrow draws with large boulders in the general area where he had come from. It was also no place for a horse indicating he must have left his horse some distance away from Jake's camp.

"Care for a cup of coffee," Jake said. "I have an extra cup in my saddlebags."

"Sounds good."

Jake turned his back on the man then knelt down next to his saddlebags. His ears were attuned to the sounds of the night. It was very quiet, not even a breeze to rustle a leaf.

As he reached for the saddlebags, he heard the unmistakable sound of a gun hammer being cocked. He quickly pushed himself backwards and to one side while drawing his gun. He quickly swung his gun around as he fell backwards, firing it at the man just as the man fired at him.

Two guns firing at the same time filled the silence of the late evening dusk with the loud sound of gunshots. One bullet hit the ground only inches from its target, while the other hit its target. One shot hit the man a few inches above and to the right of his belt buckle, just below his lower ribs. Jake's bullet had knocked the man back against a tree where he ended up lying on the ground. Jake still had his gun on the man as the man fell, and he was ready to shoot again if necessary.

When the man came to rest on the ground, his gun was off to one side of him. The man didn't move.

Jake stood up and walked over to him. He quickly took the man's rifle and pistol and moved them away from the man before he rolled him over. The man looked up at Jake. It was easy to see that he would not live very long. He had been gut shot.

"What's your name?" Jake asked.

The man just looked at him for a moment before he spoke. "Dwight Anderson," he said.

It was clear that Dwight was in a great deal of pain. The blood on his shirt was a bright red indicating the bullet had hit his liver. It would only be a matter of time before he would die, and there was nothing Jake could do to help him.

"Did you hold up the freight stations and kill the managers?"

"Yes," Dwight said softly.

"Did you have any help?"

"Yes."

"Who helped you?"

"A freight hauler," he said then coughed.

"What's his name?"

"Sam Mar - -," he said.

There was quiet once again. Dwight's face showed the pain he was feeling. His breath came in short, shallow gasps for only a couple of minutes before he stopped breathing.

Jake looked around and took a deep breath. He was disappointed that he had not been able to get more information out of him. Jake looked at the body, then began to think about him.

Dwight had to have a horse somewhere, or a camp nearby. It was already too dark to go wondering around away from the fire looking for his horse. He could have left it some distance away so the horse would not give away his approach to the fire.

Jake decided to cover him with a blanket, have a cup of coffee then get some rest. He would look for Dwight's horse in the morning.

After he covered the man and had his cup of coffee, Jake moved over next to a big tree and leaned back against it. He watched as his fire burned down and finally went out. He then closed his eyes and drifted off to sleep.

When morning came, Jake started looking for Dwight's horse. It didn't take him very long to find it. It was tied to a tree only about a hundred yards behind the outcropping. It had eaten all the grass around the base of the tree. Jake took the horse to the small clearing where he hobbled the horse and let it graze and drink from the spring while he had breakfast.

As soon as he finished his breakfast and put out the fire, Jake saddled his horse and packed up his things. After putting Dwight's body over his horse, Jake went to his horse and swung into the saddle. He took the reins of Dwight's horse and began the long trek back to Custer City.

Jake rode down the main street of Custer City to the sheriff's office with a man slung over the saddle. The sheriff saw him coming and stepped out of his office to meet Jake.

"What have you got there?" Sheriff Metcalf asked.

"It's Dwight Anderson. He's the man who killed the freight station managers and killed the woman in the street."

"Are you sure?"

"Yes. He told me he was the one who did it, just before he died. The young boy was right, he had one of those fancy nickel-plated pistols in his holster. And as you can see, his horse has three stocking feet and a diamond shaped blaze on his head."

"I guess the reward is yours," Sheriff Metcalf said.

"One other thing you should know. He told me how he knew what freight stations and stagecoaches to hit. He got his information from a freight hauler. Sam something."

"Sam Martin?" the sheriff asked.

"Yes. I believe that was what he was trying to say. He died before he could tell me his full last name."

"He's here in town right now. He's mean and very fast with a gun."

"Want a little help getting him?" Jake asked.

"I sure could use it. I ain't near as fast as he is," the sheriff admitted.

"Let's go get him. We can take care of Dwight later."

The sheriff nodded that he agreed. Jake and the sheriff started down the street toward the freight station. They could see Sam helping to unload a freight wagon in front of the freight station.

"That's Sam. The one in buckskins at the back of the wagon," the sheriff said.

Sam lifted a box from the back of the wagon, then turned to set it on the boardwalk in front of the freight station. Sam had just picked up another box when he turned and saw Jake and Sheriff Metcalf walking down the street toward him.

Sam froze for a moment. He could also see Dwight's horse behind them and the body draped over the horse's saddle. Seeing Dwight's horse, Sam was sure it was

Dwight across the saddle. From the look on Jake's and Sheriff Metcalf's faces, he had a feeling they were coming to get him. He realized that Dwight must have talked before he died.

Sam dropped the box and reached for his gun, but he was not fast enough. Jake drew his gun and fired it just as Sam fired his gun. Jake's bullet caught Sam in his right shoulder and spun him around causing him to drop his gun.

Sheriff Metcalf had been hit in the leg by the bullet from Sam's gun and fell to the ground. Jake turned and knelt down next to Sheriff Metcalf. He had no more than knelt down to help the sheriff when the sheriff pushed Jake away.

Jake had seen the look on the sheriff's face and immediately swung around. He saw Sam turning toward him with a gun in his hand. Jake fired a shot at Sam before Sam could shoot again. Jake's bullet hit Sam in the chest. Sam dropped to the ground. He was dead.

As soon as Jake was sure they were not in any danger, he turned around and wrapped his bandana around the sheriff's leg, then helped him to the doctor's office above the general store. While the sheriff was being taken care of by the doctor, Jake took Dwight and Sam to the undertaker. He then took Dwight's horse to the livery stable where the stable owner would take care of it until they could figure out what to do with the horse.

Jake went back to the doctor's office to check on the sheriff. He found the sheriff resting on the couch. The doctor was sitting at his desk.

"How's he doing, Doc?"

"He'll be laid up for a few days, but he's going to be okay. The bullet didn't hit any major blood vessels or any bones."

"That's good."

"Hey, thanks for saving my butt," the sheriff called out from the couch.

"Thanks for saving mine," Jake said.

"You're welcome."

"Do you need someone to help out for a few days?" Jake asked.

"No. I think my deputy can handle things as soon as he gets back."

"When's he due back?"

"Tomorrow afternoon, as far as I know. He might be back before that."

"Well, in that case I think I'll head back to Hill City," Jake said.

"Okay. I'll get the reward sent to you. If there's anything I can do for you, just let me know."

"I will. Take care," Jake said then turned and left the doctor's office.

Jake walked down the street to the sheriff's office, untied his horse from the hitching rail. He looked up at the sky and decided it was too late for him to get back to Hill City before dark. Besides, his horse could use a little rest.

He swung up in the saddle and rode his horse to the livery stable where he put his horse up for the night. He then walked over to the café and had dinner. After dinner, he went to the Kleemann House where he got a room for the night.

Jake was up early. He could hardly wait to see Suzanna again. He dressed then went to a café for his breakfast. After breakfast, he went to the livery stable where he saddled his horse then walked his horse down the street to the sheriff's office. He tied his horse to the hitching rail, then stepped up on the boardwalk. He tried the door and found it unlocked. He went inside and found a young man sitting at the sheriff's desk.

"Good morning. You must be Jake Murdock," the young man said.

"Yeah."

"Sheriff Metcalf told me about you. I'm Charlie, Metcalf's deputy."

"Nice to meet you. How's he doing?"

"He's doin' okay. He don't like the idea of bein' laid up for awhile, but he'll be back to work long 'fore he's ready to make rounds."

"I'm sure he will. I'm going to head back to Hill City. If you need any help while Metcalf is laid up, let me know."

"I will. By the way, I got a bank draft for ya. It's the reward for gettin' the man who had been robbin' the freight stations and his partner," Charlie said.

"I didn't expect it so soon."

"It was the local banker who put up the reward. It was his wife that the guy ran over in the street," Charlie said.

Charlie reached in the center drawer of the desk and pulled out an envelope. He held it out to Jake. Jake took it and put it in his pocket.

"Ain't you even goin' ta look at it?" Charlie asked, surprised he would accept it without looking at it to make sure it was correct.

"I know how much it's for. No need to look at it," Jake said with a smile. "I best be going."

"I'm sure Metcalf would like to see ya if you're ever in the area again."

"Tell him I wish him well, and that I will stop in if I get down this way again."

"Will do," Charlie said.

Jake shook Charlie's hand then turned and walked out of the sheriff's office. He untied his horse then swung into the saddle. He turned his horse and rode out of Custer City on the road to Hill City.

He let his horse gallop in the cool morning air. Jake didn't mind. He was in a hurry to see Suzanna. He could hardly wait to show her the bank draft for five hundred dollars. It would pay for some land to build a small ranch on. They could build it together.

CHAPTER FOUR

A Love Lost Forever

It was late in the afternoon when Jake arrived in Hill City. He rode up to the hitching rail in front of the Silver Dollar Saloon, stepped out of the saddle then tied his horse to the hitching rail. As he stepped up on the boardwalk, Suzanna stepped out of the saloon.

"Welcome home, stranger," she said as she stepped up in front of him. "I saw you coming up the street."

She threw her arms around his neck, raised up on her tiptoes and kissed him hard on the lips. Jake wrapped her in his arms and held her close as she kissed him. After a minute or so of welcoming him back, she loosened her hold on him and looked up into his eyes.

"I have good news for you," he said as she smiled up at him.

"The best news is you are safe and back here with me. I have missed you. Let's go to my room. We can talk there."

"Okay," Jake said as he took her arm.

They went up to Suzanna's room. Jake showed her the bank draft for the capture of Dwight Anderson. They spent some time talking about what they might do with it.

After two hours of welcoming him home, Jake left Suzanna's room, took his bank draft to the bank and deposited it, then took his horse over to the livery stable for a good rubdown and some rest.

After making sure his horse was taken care of, Jake stopped by the marshal's office to see how John was doing. John was sitting in his office watching out the window.

"Welcome back," John said as Jake walked in.

"How are you doing?" Jake asked.

"I've missed having you around to help out. How did things go for you?

"I got the man who killed the woman and the station manager."

"Good. Are you coming back to work for me?

"If I still have a job here."

"You still have a job here. How about starting first thing in the morning?"

"Sure thing."

"Okay, see you tomorrow."

Jake turned and left the marshal's office. He returned to the Silver Dollar Saloon.

When Jake walked into the saloon, he saw the barkeeper was standing behind the bar. There were two men at the end of the bar talking to each other. Jake was walking toward the staircase on his way to Suzanna's room when the barkeeper spoke.

"Welcome back, Jake."

The two men at the bar turned sharply and looked at Jake. They didn't say anything, but they looked Jake over as if sizing him up.

"Thanks," Jake replied."

"How did it go in Custer? I hear you went after the man who killed that woman and robbed the freight stations."

"I caught the man who robbed the freight stations and the man who helped him."

"Were there only two involved?" the barkeeper asked with surprise.

"As far as we know. Why, have you heard something different?" Jake asked a bit concerned.

"I had a couple of teamsters in here a couple of days ago. They were talking about four men, the one who did the robbin', two who worked at the different freight stations, and a fourth man who checked out the freight stations then planned the robberies. If you got two of them that means there are still two others out there. You might want to watch your back."

"Thanks for the information, and the warning," Jake said, looking at the barkeeper with a concerned look on his face.

Jake turned around and headed up the stairs to Suzanna's room. Once inside her room, Suzanna turned, put her arms around his neck and looked into his eyes. He kissed her then picked her up and took her to her bed. He laid her on the bed, then joined her on the bed.

After spending some time making love, Suzanna laid with Jake in the bed. He told her that he was going to start working tomorrow. They would have until tomorrow all to themselves. Jake and Suzanna spent the afternoon talking about their future and just being close. The sun had gone down and it was almost dark outside when Jake decided that he needed to get something to eat.

"I'm hungry," Jake said. "I haven't had anything to eat since early this morning."

"Would you like to go to the café for dinner?" Suzanna asked.

"Sure."

"Give me a minute to get ready," Suzanna said as she stood up.

Jake got out of bed and dressed then sat on the settee while he waited for Suzanna to get dressed. As soon as she was ready, they left her room and went downstairs. When they got to the bottom of the stairs, the barkeeper motioned for Jake to come over to the bar. He let go of Suzanna's arm and walked over to the bar.

"What's up, Ralph?"

"Did ya notice the two men standin' at the end of the bar when ya came in earlier?" the barkeeper asked.

"I saw them, but didn't pay any attention to them. Why?"

"I've never seen them before, but I saw the way they looked at ya. They didn't seem none too happy that you was here. They talked in low whispers. I couldn't make out what they was sayin', but I'm sure they were talking about ya."

Jake thought about what the barkeeper said. He wondered who the two men were and why they might be interested in him. It even crossed his mind they might be the two men the barkeeper had told him about earlier.

"Any idea who they were?"

"No. I've never seen 'um before, but they took a good deal of interest in ya."

"I'll keep an eye out for them," Jake said. "Any idea where they went?"

"No. They left here about two hours ago. They might have left town, but I can't say for sure."

"Thanks. Suzanna and I are going across the street for dinner. We'll be back shortly."

"Be careful out there. I didn't see if they left town or not."

Jake nodded, then turned and smiled at Suzanna. He walked to Suzanna then took her by the arm and walked to the door. He held the door for Suzanna then followed her out onto the boardwalk in front of the saloon.

As he stepped up beside her, Jake saw a flash of light just as he heard a shot fired. He was suddenly struck by a bullet that had come from between the buildings across the street. The shot that was fired hit Jake's left arm. Jake managed to draw his gun and return fire. Several shots were exchanged, but it was over in just a few seconds. He heard the sounds of someone running down the alley behind the café.

Jake turned to see if Suzanna was all right just as Ralph came out of the door with a shotgun in his hands. Jake found her lying on the boardwalk. There was blood on the front of her dress.

Jake knelt down and took Suzanna in his arms. He was still holding her when John came running toward him with a gun in his hand. Jake looked up at John.

From the look on Jake's face, John knew Suzanna was dead. John stood there, not knowing what to say.

After several minutes, people began to gather around. Jake picked Suzanna up in his arms and carried her into the saloon. He took her up the stairs to her room and laid her on the bed they had shared just a short time earlier.

John had followed Jake into Suzanna's room. He stood by for a moment or two before he turned and left the room. John went down the street and got Doc Wilson. He returned to Suzanna's room with the doctor.

"Jake, Doc needs to look at your arm," John said.

Jake did not respond. Doc Wilson stepped up beside Jake.

"Jake, you're going to have to take your shirt off."

Without taking his eyes off Suzanna, Jake removed his shirt. Doc sat down beside him and cleaned the wound. It had to have been painful, yet Jake never even flinched. Doc dressed the wound then stood up. He looked at John before he spoke to Jake.

"It was a pretty clean wound. Your arm will be stiff for a few days and hurt if you try to use it, but you should have complete recovery in a couple of weeks," Doc said to Jake.

Doc was sure Jake had not heard a word he said. He looked at John, then stood up to leave.

"Thanks, Doc," John said.

"See if you can get him to listen to you. He needs to take care of that arm. I'll talk to you later," Doc said.

"I'll tell him what you said, Doc."

Doc nodded then turned and left the room.

It wasn't long before John left Jake alone with Suzanna. Jake spent the night sitting by the bed where

Suzanna laid. He never left her side, never shed a tear and never fell asleep.

Early the next morning, John and a couple of other men came to Suzanna's room. Two of the men waited at the door to her room while John went inside. John walked up next to Jake.

"Jake, it's time to put her to rest," he said softly.

Jake looked up at his friend for a moment. He didn't say anything, he simply nodded his head that he understood. Jake stood up, stepped back and watched John and one of the other men carefully wrap Suzanna in the quilt from her bed. They put her on a stretcher and carried her to the doctor's office. Jake followed them, but said nothing.

Once inside the doctor's office, the men gently placed Suzanna in a coffin made of pine. Jake watched as they put the lid on the coffin. Two other men joined them. Four of the town's men carried the coffin down the street to the cemetery while Jake followed along behind with Doc on one side of him and John on the other. A couple of the working women from the Silver Dollar Saloon joined them.

When they arrived at the cemetery, Jake stood next to the grave that had been dug earlier that morning and watched as they lowered the coffin into the ground.

The local preacher had been waiting for them at the cemetery. He said a few words from the Good Book. Each of the women from the saloon tossed a flower in on top of the coffin before two of the men started to fill the grave.

After the preacher and all the others had left, John and Jake stood next to the grave. Jake looked up at the sky. John stood beside him, but didn't say a word. He just wanted to be there for his friend.

Suddenly, Jake turned to John. He didn't say anything for several minutes before he spoke.

"Thank you, John, for all you have done for me. Now I need to do something for myself."

"What are you going to do? The Doc says you have to take care of that arm."

"I know. I'm going to find the men who killed her," he said without any sign of emotion.

John didn't say anything, he knew what Jake was going to do. He also knew there was no way he could stop Jake even if he wanted to, which he didn't. He wanted the men who had shot her to pay with their lives.

Jake turned and walked back toward the saloon. He went to Suzanna's room and gathered his belongings then went to the livery stable. He saddled his horse then led the horse out of the stable. He walked the horse to the space between the two buildings where the shots had been fired that killed Suzanna.

Jake took his time as he carefully walked around the area looking for something that would help him find the shooters. It didn't take him but a few minutes to find signs of blood on the ground. There were the tracks of two men in the dirt. He was now sure he had hit at least one of them during the shootout. He had no idea how badly the man was hurt, but he really didn't care. If it was up to him, the shooters would hurt a lot more before they died.

Jake began slowly following the blood trail and the footprints, leading his horse behind him. The trail left by two men went behind several of the buildings, but came to an end near a tree behind the general store. There he found the tracks of two horses that had been tied to the tree. The horses had apparently been there for some time because all the grass at the base of the tree had been chewed to the ground.

He studied the hoof prints very carefully for several minutes so he could follow them wherever they went. From the looks of the tracks, the two men had mounted up and rode off in a hurry. Jake looked off in the direction the tracks indicated the two men had gone.

Jake took a deep breath, then swung into the saddle and began following the tracks. Since the two were in a big hurry to get away from town, it was easy for Jake to follow them. They were headed in a northerly direction, but stayed off any of the most commonly used roads heading north. He had no idea where they might be going, but he didn't care. All he knew was they had almost a day's head start, but that didn't matter either. Jake would follow them into hell, if necessary.

It wasn't long before Jake found a place where the men had stopped. Their horses had been tied to a tree and all the grass had been eaten around the tree. That, along with all the tracks, indicated they had stopped to rest and had been there for some time. The footprints in the dirt indicated they had gotten off their horses, but they hadn't gone far. They had walked over to a tree that had fallen a good many years ago. It was clear that they had sat on it.

He found several pieces of cloth with dried blood on them. The only thing Jake could make of it was they had stopped to rest and dress the wounds of the one he had apparently shot. They had probably spent the night there, but didn't build a fire for fear that it might be seen or smelled by someone.

Jake turned and looked back at the tree where they had tied their horses. He slowly walked back looking for tracks in the dirt. The tracks showed that both of them had returned to their horses and continued on toward the north.

Jake returned to his horse and swung into the saddle. He again started out following the trail they were leaving. After several hours, he noticed blood on the leaves of a small scrub oak that was close to the narrow trail they had been following. It was clear that one of them was still bleeding. Jake doubted that he would last very much longer before he bled to death.

Several hours later, Jake found himself looking down on the small town of Silver City. He looked at the town in the valley below and wondered if the men he was after went there. Their tracks seemed to point in that direction. He nudged his horse on down the narrow road toward the town. He kept a sharp lookout for anybody who might cause him harm.

Staying alert to his surroundings, Jake rode his horse toward the town. He stopped at the edge of town and took note of the horses that were tied to the hitching railings. He had no idea what their horses looked like, but he might discover where they went.

Jake had just entered the edge of town when he reined up his horse again. He looked around again before stepping out of the saddle. Jake reached down and lifted his gun from his holster then eased it back into place. He wanted it setting lightly in the holster so it could be drawn as quickly and smoothly as possible.

After taking a deep breath, he began walking down the street, leading his horse. As he walked past the saloon, two men stepped out on the boardwalk. He turned sharply toward them and was ready to draw, but quickly realized they were not the men he was after. They were unarmed and looked like they might be prospectors.

He turned back and slowly continued to walk down the street. He looked at each horse as he walked by them. It wasn't until he came to one horse with several rather dark smudged spots on the saddle and on the horse's side. Jake looked around to make sure no one was watching him, then walked up next to the horse. The spots were wet and a dark red. He reached out and touched one of the larger spots, then looked at his fingers. There was no doubt in his mind that the spots were blood, and it was fresh. He reached out and slide his hand under the saddle and touched the horse's back. The horse's back was damp. Jake knew the horse had been ridden recently.

Jake stepped away from the horse, then walked a little further down the street. He tied his horse to a hitching rail on the same side of the street as the horse he had just checked, then moved up close to the building. He leaned against the building to wait, look around and think.

He was sure the horse with the bloody saddle belonged to one of the men he was after, but where were they? Where had they gone?

Looking up and down the street, Jake noticed a small sign at the end of the building with an arrow painted on it. The sign pointed up alongside the building and read simply "Doctor".

It was clear that at least the man he had shot in Hill City was in the doctor's office. The real question was, where was the other one? There was only the one horse in front of the Doctor's office. Had he left town leaving his partner in the doctor's care, or was he in the doctor's office with his partner just waiting to see if they had been followed? If he was with his partner, where was his horse?

Jake noticed the doctor's office was right across the street from a café. He decided to go across the street and get something to eat while watching the doctor's office from the café.

Keeping his eyes moving to avoid being surprised, he stepped off the boardwalk then hurried across the street and quickly entered the café. He found an empty table near a window which would allow him to keep an eye on the doctor's office and most of the main street of the town while he got something to eat.

When the waitress came to his table, Jake ordered a meal. It didn't take very long before she returned and put a plate of steak and eggs in front of him. She returned a second time with a cup of coffee. She had just set the cup on the table when a bullet smashed through the window shattering the cup, splattering pieces of the cup and the coffee all over the table.

Jake grabbed the waitress and pulled her to the floor close to the wall. He pushed her behind him then creeped over to the edge of the window.

Jake drew his gun then stood up against the wall next to the window. He peered around the edge of the window in an effort see where the shot had come from, but saw nothing except a few people running for cover in the local shops.

It wasn't difficult for Jake to figure out where the shot had come from. With the angle of the shot through the table, it was easy to see that the shot had come from the second story of the building across the street. He watched the windows on the second story. He didn't know if there was a backway out, but he continued to look at the windows and glanced at the space between the buildings.

Time passed slowly. He was beginning to think that he was going to have to dig the shooter out of the building across the street, but to do so could prove to be difficult as well as dangerous. It could also prove to be a bad decision. Jake turned and looked at the waitress lying on the floor looking at him, her eyes big with the look of fear in them.

"Is there a backdoor to this place," he asked.

"Yes," the waitress said looking scared.

"Stay down until you see someone come out of the store across the street."

The waitress simply looked at him and nodded that she understood.

Jake moved cautiously to the back of the café and slipped out the backdoor. He ran down behind a couple of shops, then worked his way to the front corner of the last shop. Jake peeked around the corner. When he didn't see anyone on the street, he quickly ran across the street and took cover at the corner of a building. He worked his way along the side of the building to the back. Looking around he saw a man run out of the back of the building where the doctor's office was located and jump on a horse.

Jake stepped out from the corner, aimed his pistol at the man running away from him and fired. His bullet hit the man in the arm, but didn't knock him off his horse. The man ducked around the corner of a building before Jake could shoot again.

Running back out to the street, he got there in time to see the man disappear around another corner. He was heading out of town as fast as his horse could carry him. Jake ran to his horse, jumped in the saddle and gave chase.

Jake found it easy to follow the man who had fired at him. His horse was kicking up a trail of dust and dirt. When Jake came to a long stretch of straight road, he could see he had gained on the shooter.

It was also apparent to the shooter that Jake was closing in on him. The shooter was leaning forward on his horse and whipping him with the end of the reins in an effort to get the horse to run faster, but the horse was going as fast as it could. Even without whipping his horse on, Jake's horse was still gaining on the shooter.

The man knew Jake would be close enough to start shooting at him in a matter of minutes. He needed to find someplace where he could find cover.

As the shooter followed the road around a turn, he spotted a narrow trail off to the side. He reined in his horse, then turned onto the narrow trail. He had not gone far when he came to several large boulders that looked like they might provide him with some cover. The man reined up his horse and jumped out of the saddle. He grabbed his rifle then ran in among the boulders leaving his horse to just wander off.

The man had just gotten in among the boulders, when a shot was fired that ricocheted off one of the boulders. He ducked down just as he saw Jake disappear in among the trees on the other side of the narrow trail. With the thick underbrush near the edge of the trail and the rather larger pines growing in the area, the man could not see where Jake had gone.

Jake could see the man looking around over the top of a large boulder in an effort to figure out where he had gone. Jake took his time looking over the situation. He studied the rock formation and boulders around it. It would be hard for Jake to get around behind the shooter, but it would also be hard for the shooter to figure out where Jake was hiding.

The shooter had found cover in a place where he couldn't go anywhere without putting himself in danger of being shot by Jake. He had trapped himself in among the rocks. There was nothing else he could do but try to get a good shot at Jake.

"Are you ready to give up? You've got no place to go," Jake called out to him.

"So you can hang me? Not on your life." the shooter responded.

Jake looked out from his position in the bushes. He noticed there were several boulders directly behind the man. Jake thought about ricocheting a couple of bullets off the boulders. He also knew that each shot he took would give away his position. From what he could see of the man, the man had no idea of Jake's current position.

After looking around, Jake decided to shoot at the boulders, then roll away from his position and get set to shoot again as quickly as possible. Maybe he would get a good shot at the man. If nothing else, he could make it very uncomfortable for him.

Jake aimed his rifle at a spot on the rock right above and behind where he had last seen the man's head. He slowly squeezed the trigger until the rifle fired. Rolling over as quickly as possible, he reset himself to shoot again. Jake again fired a shot at the rock, then moved again. He repeated the 'shoot and move' several times before he stopped.

The man hunkered down as pieces of rock from the boulder above and behind him fell down on him with each shot. Some of the pieces hit him fairly hard, but all of them kept him pinned down so he was unable to return fire, or to see where Jake had moved. The rain of pieces of rock on the man's head and back was also nerve racking, as well as frightening.

From Jake's new position, he could see the man had hunkered down. This was his chance. As Jake reloaded his rifle to prepare for his next move, six shots from a pistol were fired into the bushes from the boulder, but none of them came close to where Jake was hiding.

When the shooting stopped, Jake looked toward the boulders and saw the man's head slowly rise up over one of the boulders. Jake could only see part of the man's face as he looked around. From the movement of the man's head and the places he was looking, it was easy for Jake to see the man was scared and that he was unable to find Jake.

The more the man looked around, the more he exposed himself. Jake thought the man might think he had hit him. Jake waited, not making a sound or moving. He just watched and waited.

Time passed slowly, and it would not be long until the sun would sink below the hills off to the west. It was getting time to end it. If it got dark, there was a chance, a slim chance, that the man could get away. Jake did not want that to happen.

Just as Jake was getting ready to shoot the man as he looked around, the man ducked back down. Jake moved about forty feet off to the left from where he had fired his last shot. There was an opening in the bushes where he could break out and run across the trail. He levered a round into the chamber of his rifle, got himself ready then stood up. Jake ran across the narrow trail, firing shot after shot into the rocks behind the man until he was only a few yards from the man.

Jake ducked behind a boulder. When he looked over the boulder, he found the man lying low with his hands covering his head from the pieces of rock that had fallen from the boulder behind him. Jake laid his rifle over the top of the boulder and aimed it at the man.

"Don't make a move. I have you in my sights," Jake said.

The man slowly moved his hands from over his head, then turned to look at Jake. Jake was only ten feet from him and there was no place to go.

"You can surrender to me, or you can try for your gun. I kind of hope you reach for your gun," Jake said his eyes filled with hate.

The man dropped his gun then stood up and raised his hands above his head. Jake marched him out of the boulders to his horse. He took a rope from his saddle and tied it around the man's neck. He led him to a tree, tossed the rope over a tree branch.

"Oh God, don't hang me," the man cried.

"I'm not going to hang you unless you give me a reason, any reason at all."

Jake tied the rope tight enough so the man's feet could barely touch the ground. Jake took a small piece of rope and tied the man's hands behind his back. Once he had the man secured, Jake walked down the trail and retrieved his horse and the man's horse. After tying them to a tree, he retrieved the man's guns. When Jake had gathered everything into one place, he looked at the man. He could see the fear on his face.

"What's your name," Jake asked.

"Larry Waters," he replied with a quiver in his voice.

"Who was your partner?"

"My younger brother, Jesse. He died in the doctor's office just minutes before you came into town."

"Were the two of you working with Dwight Anderson to rob freight stations and stagecoaches?"

"Yes," he said softly.

Jake turned and sat down on a log. It was going to be dark soon. He decided to wait until morning to return to Silver City. He laid out his bedroll and made himself comfortable.

"Are you going to leave me like this all night?" Larry asked, his voice showing he was afraid of what the answer might be.

"Yes. I don't want you getting lose and killing me in the middle of the night."

With that Jake rolled over on his side and went to sleep.

When morning came, Jake looked toward the tree where he had tied Larry. Larry was still there. He got up and saddled the horses, then put Larry on his horse and tied him to the saddle with the rope still around his neck. He stepped in the saddle while holding the reins of Larry's horse and the end of the rope around Larry's neck in one hand. Jake started out for Silver City.

It was shortly before noon when he rode down the street of Silver City with his prisoner, the rope still around his neck and the end of it in Jake's hand.

Jake stopped in front of the café, tying the horses to a hitching rail. Jake went inside and got a couple of rolls and some coffee. He fed Larry while he was sitting on the horse. When they were finished eating, he untied the horses, got back in the saddle and continued on to Hill City.

When Jake arrived in Hill City, he took Larry directly to the jail and turned him over to Marshal Walker. The marshal locked him up.

"I'll leave him in your hands," Jake said. "I will be leaving."

"I understand," John said. "Where are you going?"

Jake was standing next to a board on the wall that had a couple of wanted posters on it. He looked at them for a minute before he pulled one off the wall then looked at John.

"I'm going to Sturgis," he said as he folded the wanted poster, put it in his pocket and walked out the door.

John followed him as far as the door and watched him get on his horse and ride out of town. He silently wished Jake success and that someday he would find peace and happiness.

CHAPTER FIVE

The Hunt for Joseph Black Heart

Jake rode out of Hill City and headed north toward Sturgis without looking back. He didn't want to even look at Hill City, at least for a little while.

The wanted poster he took from the marshal's office in Hill City was only four days old. It was for a man who had savagely beaten and stabbed a woman to death in a local saloon in Sturgis. The woman had been working in the saloon and apparently said something, or did something, he didn't like.

The poster described the man as a half-breed who was very good with a knife. He was almost six foot tall, with a long scar on the right side of his face. He was wearing buckskin pants and shirt with some Indian beadwork on the front of the shirt, and high-top moccasins with a knife stuck in the top. He had a black hat with an eagle feather stuck in the hatband. He was last seen heading south into the Black Hills on a brown and white horse. He called himself Black Heart, Joseph Black Heart. The wanted poster offered one thousand dollars for him "dead or alive, preferably dead".

Jake took his time as he worked his way through the Black Hills toward Deadwood and Lead. If Black Heart was going south from Sturgis, he was probably headed into the Black Hills, and would probably go through Deadwood. Jake knew that it was one place where Black Heart could get supplies if he had left Sturgis in a hurry, which was probably the case after what he had done.

There were a good many places Black Heart could hide in the hills. Jake would stop in Deadwood and see if the local sheriff had seen him there. The sheriff might be able to give him some idea where Black Heart might have gone.

It took Jake two days to get to Deadwood. He arrived about two-thirty in the afternoon. Jake went directly to the sheriff's office. He rode up to the hitching rail, stepped out of the saddle and tied his horse in front of the office. As he stepped up on the boardwalk in front of the sheriff's office, he stopped and took a minute to look up and down the street before he turned and went into the office.

The sheriff was sitting at his desk and looked up at Jake as he walked in. The sheriff waited for Jake to close the door behind him before saying anything.

"What can I do for you?" the sheriff asked as he looked Jake over.

"I'm looking for this man," Jake said pulling the wanted poster out of his pocket.

Jake opened the folded wanted poster and handed it to the sheriff. He watched as the sheriff looked at it.

"You a bounty hunter?" the sheriff asked looking up at Jake.

Jake just looked at him for a moment before he answered. He wasn't sure what the sheriff thought about bounty hunters.

"Yes."

"The last time I heard about him, he was headed out of town."

"Do you know where he was going?"

"No, but from the supplies he picked up, it would be my guess he was headed out to do some huntin', probably out on the prairie."

"What makes you think he was going hunting?"

"He bought some shells for a buffalo rifle. We don't see many buffalo around here this time of year. Plus, he headed east toward the open prairie."

"You think he was headed back to his tribe?"

"I doubt it. He's not welcome at his tribe. He killed a squaw there a couple of years back. She was the daughter of one of the tribe's chiefs. I was told by one of the chiefs that if he ever showed his face in their encampment, he would not live but a few very painful hours," the sheriff said with a slight grin.

"I would guess there are very few places he could go without someone wanting to kill him," Jake said.

"I would agree with you on that. He sure ain't welcome here. You still plannin' on goin' after him?"

"Yes. How is it you didn't arrest him while he was here?"

"I didn't know he was here until the shopkeeper at the general store told me that he saw him leavin' town. The shopkeeper also told me what he bought."

"What road did he take out of town?"

"He didn't. According to the shopkeeper, Black Heart took an old trail used by Indians years ago. It goes almost straight east. It ain't used much and it ain't all that easy to find. If you plan on trailin' him, you best be very careful. There's a lot of places where he can ambush you on that trail," the sheriff warned.

"Thanks for the warning. Where do I find this old Indian trail?"

"You can find it about a hundred yards, or so, past the city limits on the Sturgis Road. There's a gap in a couple of big rocks on the east side of the road. You'll need to be lookin' for it. It ain't easy to see."

"How long ago did he leave?"

"It was yesterday about two or two-thirty in the afternoon."

"He's about a day ahead of me," Jake said thoughtfully. "Thank you. I best be going."

"You be careful out there. That half-breed is mean and he's tough."

"Thanks. I'll keep that in mind," Jake said then turned and left the sheriff's office.

Once outside, Jake again looked up and down the street. It was getting on toward three o'clock. He walked his horse down the street toward the General Store. He tied his horse in front of the store then went inside.

After getting some supplies and putting them in his saddlebags, he swung into the saddle and headed out of town toward the trail Black Heart was reported to have taken. As soon as he arrived at the old Indian trail, he stopped and looked down the trail for a minute. He wondered if he was riding into hell by taking the old Indian trail. All he had to go on was what the sheriff had told him, and it wasn't very encouraging. There was no way for him to know if he was riding into a trap. As far as he knew, Black Heart didn't know anyone was after him, but he might have thought that someone would be hunting him simply because of what he had done in Sturgis.

Jake took a moment to study the tracks in the dirt. As far as he could tell, there had been only one horse using the trail recently. The tracks showed it was an unshod horse, and that no effort had been made to cover the tracks. The fact that the horse was unshod led Jake to believe it was probably Black Heart's horse that had made the hoof prints in the dirt. Jake decided he would follow the tracks for a little while in the hope of discovering if Black Heart knew or thought he was being followed.

Nudging his horse onto the trail, Jake rode along as if they were out for a casual Sunday ride with no destination in mind. As he rode along the trail, Jake would casually look down to make sure the trail left by the unshod horse had not changed. Any change in the hoof prints might indicate that Black Heart had discovered he was being followed, or at the very least, he might think he was being followed.

Jake took his time. He did not want Black Heart to know that he was being followed. It was Jake's plan to find Black Heart before Black Heart discovered he was even there.

It was getting on toward sunset when Jake noticed a second set of hoof prints that came onto the trail from the woods and headed in the same direction that Black Heart had gone. The second set of hoof prints were from an unshod horse as well. Jake wondered if another Indian had come onto the trail, and if the second Indian was hunting Black Heart, or if he simply joined up with Black Heart.

Jake reined up and looked down the trail for a moment before he stepped out of the saddle for a closer look at the tracks. Holding the reins of his horse in one hand, he knelt down to closely examine the two sets of hoof prints. He took a minute to compare the tracks. The second set of tracks were over the first set. Every flaw in the first set of tracks matched perfectly with the second set. There was also a place where the horse had stood for a short time before moving onto the trail.

Jake looked on down the trail and began to smile. It was clear to him what Black Heart had done. He would ride for a ways, then he would circle around to see if there were any other tracks over his. If there were, he would know he was being followed. If there were no new tracks, he would know that he was not being followed.

Jake looked up at the sky. It would be dark before long. Tracking someone like Black Heart would be extremely difficult and dangerous, if not impossible in the dark. It was time to find a place where he could set up camp. He swung back into the saddle, rode off the trail and started looking for a place not too far off the trail where he could build a small fire to fix his dinner and then sack out for the night.

He rode off the trail on the opposite side from the tracks that came onto the trail. If nothing else, it would give Black Heart the idea that the shod horse was not trailing him. Jake didn't have to go very far to find a place in among the rocks where he could set up camp.

The place where Jake decided to set up camp had some fairly high rocks on three sides. They were high enough to block off any sight of a fire. The evening breeze was coming out of the south. It would make the smoke and the smell of a fire drift away from the direction Black Heart had gone.

There was also a small area of grass that would provide grazing for Jake's horse. He hobbled his horse in the grass, took the saddle off the horse and carried it to a place where he felt he could get some rest. He laid out his bedroll where he could easily see his horse, then built a small almost smokeless fire. He fixed dinner, then brewed a pot of coffee. When he had finished his dinner, he poured himself a cup of coffee, then sat down on his bedroll and leaned back against his saddle while he watched the fire burn itself out.

By the time darkness began to cover the land, the fire had burned down to just a few coals. Jake poured himself another cup of coffee from the small coffee pot then dumped the rest over the coals. He checked on his horse, then drew his rifle from the saddle scabbard and laid it next to him on his bedroll under his blanket. Jake took off his gun belt and hung it over the saddle horn, but put the pistol close to his side in easy reach under his blanket.

As he laid on his bedroll with his head resting on his saddle and his gun in his hand, he listened to the sounds of the night. He could hear the sounds of the breeze in the few leafy trees that where nearby, his horse chomping on the grass, and an owl in a tree a short distance away. All seemed to be as it should. Jake pulled his blanket up over him, then closed his eyes in the hope of getting some sleep. It wasn't long and he was asleep.

Jake's sleep was suddenly disturbed by the sound of something behind a large rock. His eyes flew open only to discover that it was still dark. However, the sky was starting to lighten off to the east allowing just a hint of light on the rocks.

He slowly turned his head from side to side in an effort to see where the noise was coming from, but it was still too dark to see much of anything. As quietly as possible, Jake rolled out from under his blanket. With his pistol in hand, he carefully moved away from his bedroll. Jake worked his way around so he could see behind a large rock. He stood up and smiled to himself when he noticed some leaves behind the rock were moving. Some small critter was digging around in the leaves looking for something to eat. Jake looked at his horse and found it looking at him.

"A lot of good you are," he said to the horse.

Jake moved back to where he had laid out his bedroll and sat down on it. He looked up at the sky as he thought about what he was doing. Just the thought that Black Heart had a buffalo rifle made him wonder what he was going to do with it. Was he really going hunting or did he have another use for such a long range rifle. The fact he knew so little about Black Heart was enough to make him want to be extra careful.

Since he was not going to get any more rest, Jake decided to get up. He got up and gathered a few small branches to use for a fire. Once his fire was going well, he cooked a few thick slices of bacon and baked a couple of dough biscuits. As soon as they were ready, he ate his breakfast. He then gave his horse some water before he saddled it.

After packing up his supplies and bedroll, he swung into the saddle. He rode back to the trail and began following the tracks left by the unshod horse. It wasn't very long before he came to the place where the unshod horse had left the trail to circle back. There was once again only one set of unshod hoof prints left on the trail for him to follow. The more he thought about the trail he was following, the more he began to wonder where Black Heart was going.

It was mid-afternoon when Jake came to the edge of the forest. He reined up his horse and sat looking out over the open plains. He could see where the trail wandered out into the open prairie.

While still sitting in the saddle, he leaned back to get his field glasses from his saddlebags when a bullet whizzed by skipping across the top of the saddle horn. It was followed by the loud crack of rifle fire. Jake dove for the ground and his horse ran off for a short distance.

After hugging the ground for a moment, Jake turned around and crawled through the tall grass to a shallow ravine only a few feet from where he dropped to the ground. He felt like kicking himself for not grabbing his rifle before he dove off the saddle. From the time the bullet struck his saddle until he heard the report of the rifle, he knew that the shot had come from some distance away, much further away than a pistol could reach with any degree of accuracy.

Once in the ravine, Jake took a moment to catch his breath then took off his hat. Without raising his head too high, he looked around. He could see his horse standing in the tall grass looking off to the south. He was looking toward where the shot had come from, generally south of Jake's position.

Jake took a moment to look at his immediate surroundings. He quickly noticed that the ravine he was in ran almost straight east. Bent down to avoid being seen, Jake began to run along the bottom of the ravine with his gun in one hand and his hat in the other. Once he had gone about a hundred yards, he stopped and crawled up to the rim of the ravine. He slowly rose up and looked out over the area in the hope of seeing Black Heart.

The one thing he noticed was the ravine Black Heart had shot at him from was slightly higher than the one he was in, which gave Black Heart the advantage. He also noticed that further out on the prairie, the ravines almost came together.

While he looked at the ravine where Black Heart had shot from, he could see the head of Black Heart's horse. That gave Jake a pretty good idea of where Black Heart was hiding. He could also make out the top of Black Heart's black hat with the feather in it. From the way it was pointed, it looked as if Black Heart was still looking in the direction of where Jake had been when he dove off his horse.

Jake drew back from the top of the ravine. He began moving along the bottom of the ravine toward where the two ravines came together. When he was close to where the ravines came together, he crawled up and looked over the edge of the ravine again. Jake could see Black Heart's hat. He noticed that it was turning first one way then the other. It was clear that Black Heart still didn't know where Jake was located. It was also clear that Jake had not gotten any closer to Black Heart.

Suddenly, Black Heart stood up and ran to his horse. He jumped up on the back of his horse and started riding along the ravine and away from where Jake dove off his horse. The only thing was, Black Heart was actually riding closer to where Jake was lying in the grass.

When Black Heart got within pistol range, Jake stood up and fired several shots. Black Heart leaned down on his horse as he turned the animal away from Jake and rode off as fast as his horse could carry him.

Jake fired a couple of more shots at Black Heart. He noticed that Black Heart seemed to lose his balance for just a moment before he recovered. Jake wasn't sure, but he might have hit Black Heart. If he did, it didn't do enough damage that it caused Black Heart to fall off his horse.

Jake stood on the rim of the ravine and watched as Black Heart disappeared in the distance. As soon as Black

Heart was out of sight, Jake turned and looked for his horse. The animal was standing in the grass about fifty yards away. Jake began walking toward his horse. While walking toward his horse, he reloaded his pistol then slipped it into his holster.

When Jake got to his horse, he grabbed the reins and swung into the saddle. He nudged the horse toward where he thought he might have hit Black Heart with one of the shots he had fired. When he got to the spot where he thought he hit Black Heart, he was surprised to see a buffalo rifle lying on the ground.

He stopped and stepped out of the saddle. Jake reached down and picked up the rifle. He found that it was loaded. Jake also found that it had blood on it. He looked off in the direction that Black Heart had gone. Jake wondered where he would go to lick his wounds. From what the sheriff in Deadwood had said, Jake doubted that Black Heart would go to his tribe.

Jake returned to his horse. He tied the buffalo rifle to his saddle, then swung into the saddle. As he started to follow Black Heart, he found blood on several blades of grass. As he continued to follow the tracks left by the half-breed, he continued to find blades of grass with blood on them. It soon became apparent that one of his bullets did a bit of damage to Black Heart. With the amount of blood Jake was seeing, he believed it would not be long before Black Heart would have to stop and care for his wound, or he would fall off his horse as he grew weaker due to a lack of blood. If he did not take care of his wound, he was sure to bleed to death.

Jake made it a point to keep his eyes moving as he followed the blood trail in the grass. He had trailed Black Heart for several miles before the blood trail ended. There was still the trail that Black Heart's horse was leaving in the tall grass.

Jake continued to follow that trail. He moved slowly hoping that he would see Black Heart before the half-breed saw him. He had no idea where Black Heart was going. It seemed as if his horse was moving across the prairie with no destination in mind.

After tracking the horse for a couple of miles, he got a glimpse of the horse as it went over a small rise. The horse was a long way ahead. Jake pulled up and reached for his field glasses in his saddlebag. He put them up to his eyes and looked toward the horse. He was surprised at what he saw, he lowered the field glasses then put them up to his eyes again. Jake saw the same thing. The horse was walking almost straight east, but there was no rider on the horse.

Jake looked around for some sign of Black Heart, but saw nothing. He put the field glasses up to his eyes again and slowly scanned the area. He was looking for anything that would give him some idea where Black Heart might be. Since he had not had the horse in sight for most of the time he was tracking it, he believed Black Heart could be almost anywhere. He had not seen any signs of a place where Black Heart had gotten off or had fallen off his horse.

With the tall grass that covered the prairie, Jake knew that he would have to be very careful. Black Heart could be just about anywhere. Since Jake didn't know how badly Black Heart was injured, he would have to be especially careful.

Jake looked off to his right and then to his left. Off to his left, there was a rise in the ground that would give him a better view of the area. It wasn't very far. He turned his horse and rode up to the higher ground. Once on the hilltop, he swung out of the saddle, took his field glasses and again scanned the area. This time, he scanned it very slowly as he looked for anything that might give him some idea where Black Heart had gone.

One of the things he saw from the hilltop was what looked like a narrow creek with water in it that flowed in a southerly direction across the prairie below. The creek was about four hundred yards in front of him.

It was obvious that Black Heart's horse had crossed the creek and continued up the other side. Jake wondered if Black Heart had fallen off his horse when the horse crossed the creek.

Jake continued to study the area along the creek with the use of his field glasses. It seemed the perfect place for Black Heart to leave his horse. With the loss of so much blood, he would surely head for water.

Jake continued to slowly scan the area along the creek. He suddenly stopped and concentrated on one small area where he thought he had seen some movement. What he saw was some movement in the tall grass alongside the creek. Not noticing any breeze, he watched the place where the grass moved wondering if it was Black Heart, or some small animal. Jake watched it for several minutes before he saw what appeared to be a moccasin. It had moved only slightly, but it was enough for him to think he had found Black Heart.

Jake was a careful man, not prone to taking unnecessary chances. He continued to watch the moccasin for a few more minutes before he saw it move again. Looking around, he found a few rocks near the top of the hill. He walked his horse to the top of the hill, took the buffalo rifle from his saddle then walked over to the rocks and laid down among them. Using the rocks to support and steady the buffalo rifle, he took aim at the moccasin. He slowly pulled the trigger until the rifle fired.

He hit the moccasin and immediately saw it disappear into the grass. He also heard a scream of pain. He knew he had hit his target. With that shot, Jake was pretty sure that Black Heart would not be going anywhere very fast, if at all.

Jake carefully moved down the hill toward the creek. He stayed well upstream from where he shot Black Heart. Once he was close to the creek, he laid down the buffalo rifle, drew his pistol and began to slowly work his way toward Black Heart.

When Jake came around a curve in the creek bed, he could see Black Heart lying at the edge of the creek. Holding his gun on him, Jake slowly moved toward him. He was ready in case there was any fight left in Black Heart.

When Jake was only about ten feet from him, Black Heart quickly rose to a sitting position and drew back his arm with his knife in it. Jake fired his pistol and shot him in the head before he could throw the knife. Black Heart died instantly.

Jake sat down on the bank of the creek and let out a sigh of relief. He had gotten the half-breed.

As soon as the tension of going after such a man wore off, he walked back up the hill and got his horse. He could see Black Heart's horse about two hundred yards away. He rode over to the horse and tossed a rope around the horse's neck and led it back to the creek.

He wrapped Black Hawk up in a blanket and put him over his horse. Jake tied the buffalo rifle to his saddle, then began the journey to Sturgis.

As soon as Jake reached Sturgis, he turned the body over to the local sheriff, collected his bounty then returned to Hill City. He hoped that John would let him work for him again.

John welcomed him back. Jake spent his days during the winter working with Marshal John Walker to keep Hill City safe.

CHAPTER SIX

Cattleman Needs Help

Spring had come to Hill City and the Black Hills. The snow had melted away and the sun was shining across the Dakota Territory. The mornings were still a little cold, but warmed up quickly during the bright sunny days.

Jake Murdock was walking along the boardwalk of main street shortly after having his lunch at Sharon's boarding house when a man stepped out of a hotel. As soon as the man was on the boardwalk, he stopped and looked up and down the street. When he saw Jake coming toward him, the man waited for Jake to come closer.

"Excuse me, deputy," the man said when Jake was close. "I was wondering if you happen to know a man by the name of Jake Murdock. I believe he lives here in Hill City."

"I'm Jake Murdock. What can I do for you?"

"You're Jake Murdock?" the man said with a surprised look on his face.

"Yes, sir."

"I'm looking for the Jake Murdock who is a bounty hunter."

"That would be me. I work once in awhile for Marshal Walker when he needs a little help. What do you want with me?"

"I was looking to hire you to do some work for me."

"Before we get into what you want me to do, what is your name, sir?"

"My name is Fredrick Stapleton. I own a large ranch north of Belle Fourche. I'm having a problem with rustlers stealing my cattle. I would like to hire you to find out who is stealing my cattle and put a stop to it."

"Okay, but I think it would be best if we discuss this somewhere other than here on the street."

"Yes. Yes, of course. We can go to my room in the hotel right now, if you don't mind, and you can spare the time."

"That would be fine."

Mr. Stapleton turned around and started back into the hotel. Jake followed him.

Mr. Stapleton was not very tall, but he was well dressed. He was wearing a suit with a matching vest. His cowboy hat was tan and didn't have any sweat marks on it. His boots were clean and looked expensive. If Jake had to guess, the man he was following had money and might very well be who he claimed to be. The idea of catching rustlers was something Jake had not done, but it wouldn't be too far out of line from what he did as a bounty hunter.

They went past the front desk and up the stairs to Mr. Stapleton's room. Once inside the room, they sat down at a table.

"I'll get right to the point," Jake said. "What makes you think that I can stop the cattle rustling on your ranch? It is really a job for the local sheriff."

"First of all, the local sheriff has too much area to cover and cannot spend the time it would take to solve the problem. The rustlers quickly round up a few head of cattle then run them across the border into the Wyoming Territory where the sheriff can't get at them.

"In your case, you don't have the problem of jurisdictions. You can hunt them down wherever they go," Stapleton said. "I have heard that you are very good at finding and capturing lawbreakers. That is what I want you to do. By hiring you, I would have someone working full time in an effort to find out who is stealing my cattle, and put a stop to it."

"Just how do you want me to stop it?" Jake asked not sure he liked what he thought Mr. Stapleton really wanted.

"You can use any means you deem necessary. I will leave that up to you."

"I don't usually do this kind of work. I go after those who are already wanted by the law."

"I can assure you that you will be paid well for your services."

"If I catch anyone stealing your cattle, I will expect them to be tried in a court of law, not by a handful of cowboys who want to hang them," Jake said then looked at Mr. Stapleton for his reaction.

"I have no problem with that," Mr. Stapleton said. "I leave it up to you how you handle it. All I want is it stopped. I'm looking for results, and at this point I don't care how you get it."

"Then you are giving me a free hand at how I deal with those stealing cattle from you?"

"That is correct."

"I will want the law to dish out any punishment. I don't want any interference from you or your ranch hands. Do I make myself clear?"

"Very clear," Mr. Stapleton said. "I find it interesting that you insist on having the rustlers tried in a court of law."

"Why is that?"

"I happen to know that you took the law into your own hands when it came to finding the men who murdered your folks."

Jake was a little surprised that he knew about that, but shouldn't have been. News like that often travels fast on the frontier. Jake thought of ways he could defend his actions at the time, but decided to let it lie instead.

"I will need five hundred dollars up front," Jake said without replying to Mr. Stapleton. "I want one thousand dollars for each one I bring to justice for cattle rustling.

"That is a little high, but it will be worth it if you are successful," Mr. Stapleton said.

"Then we have a deal?" Jake asked.

"Yes, we have a deal," Mr. Stapleton said with a smile.

"I will be there in less than two weeks, but I will not be checking in at your ranch house. I don't want anyone to know about me, or that I am working for you."

"That's fine."

Mr. Stapleton reached into his inside coat pocket and withdrew a large sum of money. He counted out five hundred dollars and handed it to Jake.

"I will contact you when I have something important to report to you. Remember, no one, not even your foreman, is to know that I'm working for you. Is that clear?" Jake asked.

"Yes, it is clear. Do you think someone who works for me is stealing my cattle?"

"No, not at this time. I have no idea who is stealing your cattle. I just don't want word to get around that I'm there looking for the rustlers, or that I'm working for you. I don't want anyone to know I'm there at all."

"I understand. I won't tell anyone that we have even talked."

"Good. I need to get back to work," Jake said as he stood up.

Mr. Stapleton stood up and reached across the table. They shook hands sealing the deal. Jake turned and left Mr. Stapleton in his room.

Jake walked down the street to the marshal's office. When he walked in the door, he found John sitting at the desk reading the newspaper. John looked up to see who had come into the office.

"Good afternoon, Jake. How's it going?"

"Pretty good. Say, do you know a man by the name of Stapleton, Fredrick Stapleton?"

"Sure. He's a big rancher up north of Belle Fourche. Why?"

"Is he an honest man?"

"As far as I know. I've never heard anything that would make me think otherwise. What's going on?" John asked as he put down the newspaper.

"He hired me to find who has been stealing his cattle and put a stop to it."

"He couldn't have picked a better man for the job. I take it you will be leaving soon?"

"Yes. I plan to leave as soon as possible. I need to get a few things done around here before I go."

"Okay. Let me know when you're ready to leave."

"I will," Jake said then turned and left the marshal's office.

Jake walked down the street to the livery stable. He bought a second horse to use as a packhorse. He also bought a pack frame for the horse. Once he was finished at the livery stable, he went to the mercantile store where he purchased all the supplies he thought he would need, including a tent.

Jake spent most of the afternoon getting everything he would need to go to Mr. Stapleton's ranch to hide out and just watch what was going on for a few days. When he was done gathering his supplies, he went to the marshal's office. He found that John had left the office. A quick look at the clock on the wall told him that John was probably making his rounds.

Kicking back in a chair, Jake began looking at the wanted posters that were lying on John's desk. He found one for a man who had robbed a bank in Belle Fourche. He smiled at the thought of it. He was going to be in that area. If someone who knew him should see him in the area and knew he was a bounty hunter, it would provide a good reason for him to be in the area. Jake folded the wanted poster and stuck it in his shirt pocket.

It also crossed his mind that it might be a way of making a few extra dollars while in the area. It suddenly occurred to him that he could ride right up to Mr. Stapleton on his ranch, show him the wanted poster and ask him if he had seen the man. Anyone standing around or was nearby would not think he was there to find the rustlers.

Jake's thoughts were interrupted when John returned to the office. He turned and looked at John.

"Well, how are things in town?" Jake asked.

"About the same, pretty quiet. It'll be this way until Saturday. You all set to head up north?" John asked as he sat down at his desk.

"Yeah. I took one of your wanted posters. It's for a man wanted for robbing the Belle Fourche bank."

"You trying to kill two birds with one stone?" John said with a chuckle.

"Maybe, but it will provide a good reason for me being in the area should anyone discover me there."

"It will certainly do that. Good thinking," John said.

"I'm going to leave first thing in the morning. I thought I would take a minute to say goodbye now. I'll be leaving at sunup."

"Well, take care of yourself. There's always a place for you here."

"Thanks. I'll keep that in mind."

Jake stood up and walked out of the office. John remained seated at his desk as he watched Jake leave. He wondered if he would see him again. John had noticed that Jake seemed to take every chance he could to get out of town. He didn't seem to want to get close to any other woman since Suzanna was killed while she was with him. John was sure Hill City reminded him of her.

Jake walked over to the boarding house, had his dinner then went upstairs to his room. He got ready for bed then turned in for the night.

Jake was up before the sun. After having breakfast at the boarding house, he walked down the street to the livery stable. He packed his supplies on his packhorse, then saddled his riding horse. He walked them out of the stable, put his foot in the stirrup and swung into the saddle. Jake took a minute to look down the street before he turned his horse around and started out of Hill City.

The days went by slowly as he worked his way north through the Black Hills. Jake made a stop in Silver City, then moved on to Deadwood. He only stayed overnight in Deadwood before heading for Spearfish.

He stopped in Spearfish only long enough to resupply for the trip to Mr. Stapleton's ranch. Jake had no intentions of stopping in Belle Fourche. In fact, he would go well around the town because he didn't want anyone to know he was even in the area.

Jake moved on past Belle Fourche. After traveling several miles north of Belle Fourche, he found a place where there were a number of trees along a stream. He found it would be fairly easy to set up a camp in among the trees that would be hard for anyone to find unless they rode up close to it. He decided that it was a good place for a base camp while he scouted out the area.

He set up his camp and covered his tent with branches to make it even harder for anyone riding by to see. He settled in for the night. Jake had chosen a place that was almost directly west of where Mr. Stapleton's ranch house was located. He would spend some time observing what was going on in the area.

Mr. Stapleton had told him the rustlers were taking his cattle into the Wyoming Territory. Jake's immediate plan was to try to find out where they were crossing into the Wyoming Territory. He would start the first thing in the morning.

Jake spent the next four days scouting out the area. He didn't see anything but a few cattle and a few antelope. The cattle were spread out as they grazed, and seemed to be doing well.

On the morning of the fifth day, Jake rolled out of his bedroll and out of his tent. He looked up at the sky as he stretched. The sky was overcast and looked like it might rain. He had a good breakfast, then saddled his horse. After making sure his packhorse had plenty of water and feed, he swung into the saddle and rode off.

After riding around the area for the past few days, Jake now had a pretty good idea how far he was from the Wyoming line. Jake had been looking for places where cattle could be taken into Wyoming with little notice, which was about any place since it was fairly wide-open rolling prairie country.

He started riding north knowing that the Wyoming line was west of him. Jake rode from one hilltop to the next as he had done for the past four days. When he would get to the top of a hill, he would take his field glasses and carefully scan the area before moving on.

When he got to the top of the third hill and began scanning the area using his field glasses, he noticed that there were a good number of cattle in the narrow valley below, possibly sixty to seventy head. He knew cattle tended to spread out when left to simply graze on the open prairie. What caught his attention was the cattle were bunched up, and there were three cowboys with the cattle.

Jake moved back off the top of the hill to avoid being seen. He tied his horse to a lonely scrub pine, then worked his way back to the top of the hill. He laid in the grass and using his field glasses, he watched what was going on. He could see three cowboys close to the cattle. It didn't take him long to figure out what was going on.

Of the three cowboys, there was one who seemed to be the leader. Jake saw him direct one of the cowboys to ride east. Jake knew that the ranch house was generally east of his location. The one who seemed to be giving direction rode up close to the remaining cowboy. He talked to the cowboy for awhile, then turned and followed the first rider who had gone east.

Jake wasn't sure what was going on, but it didn't seem right. He took a few minutes to think about it while he continued to scan the area. The only cattle Jake saw from the hilltop were the sixty or so in the small group in the bottom of the valley. He knew that Stapleton had thousands of cattle and that they were probably spread over thousands of acres of land. The question that came to Jake's mind was what was going on with the sixty or so cattle in the little valley? Time passed slowly as he continued to watch.

The lone cowboy spent his time riding slowly around the small herd of cattle, keeping the cattle fairly well bunched up. He didn't seem to be watching the cattle very closely. The cowboy seemed to spend most of his time looking around as if he was looking to see if there might be someone around, or maybe to see if there was someone watching him. The cowboy acted almost as if he was afraid someone might see him.

It was getting on toward nightfall when two cowboys rode into the valley. Jake couldn't be sure, but it looked like it was the same two who had ridden east earlier in the day. One of them rode out to where the cowboy who had been there most the day was sitting on his horse, while the other cowboy rode over to a small grove of trees part way up the hill on the other side of the little valley. The two who remained with the cattle looked as if they were talking. After a couple of minutes, the one who had been there most the day rode over to the small group of trees. He got off his horse and tied it to a tree.

The first one to go to the trees had built a small fire. It looked like they planned to be there all night. Jake could see them talking, but could not tell what they were saying.

A slight breeze had come up and it felt like it was going to rain at any moment. Jake looked up at the sky and thought for a minute. This would be the perfect time to run some cattle into the Wyoming Territory. With the rain, there would be no tracks to follow come daybreak. The three cowboys could run the cattle into Wyoming and return to work without anyone knowing they had been gone.

The only question was where were they taking the cattle? In order to sell them they would have to change the brands on them, unless they were simply taking them into Wyoming where someone else would change the brands, then sell them.

Jake decided he would have to find out where the cattle were going. He would follow them as soon as they started moving the cattle.

Time passed slowly. It was almost dark when it started to rain. It wasn't a heavy rain, but if it rained for very long it would wipe away any tracks.

Jake moved back off the top of the hill. He went to his horse, took his slicker off the saddle and put it on. He then swung into the saddle. Jake rode up close to the top of the hill. He had to wait only a few minutes before the three cowboys started to move the cattle west toward the Wyoming line.

As soon as the cattle had started to move, Jake started walking his horse in the same direction. He didn't follow them, but rode off to the side. Much of the time he could not make out the cowboys or the cattle, but he could hear the cattle as they moved west.

The rain continued all the time the cattle were being moved closer to Wyoming. Jake was sure he had it pretty well figured out. The three cowboys would drive the cattle into Wyoming, then return to work before the sun came up. If Jake was right, they wouldn't be taking the cattle very far into Wyoming. They would need time to get back to work before sunup so no one would miss them.

Shortly after the cattle crossed the Wyoming line, they came upon a cabin. Jake figured they had only gone a little over a mile into Wyoming. He watched the cattle being driven into a draw just north of the cabin. He didn't dare go any closer as he didn't want to be seen.

There was a light on in the cabin. He rode in among some trees on the south side of the cabin and watched the hill to the north.

It wasn't long and he saw someone come out of cabin and stand on the porch. It was only a few more minutes before the three cowboys rode out of the draw and up to the cabin. They got off their horses, tied them to the hitching rail in front of the cabin, then went inside with the man who had come out to greet the cowboys.

Jake knew he was taking a chance, but he stepped out of the saddle and tied his horse to one of the trees. He then snuck across the open space between the trees and the cabin. Once he was at the side of the cabin, he worked his way around to the front and looked through the window. He could not see the face of the man who was in the cabin when the cowboys arrived, but he got a good look at the three cowboys. Jake was sure that he would be able to recognize them if he saw them again.

He watched through the window as the man from the cabin counted out some money and handed it to one of the cowboys. Jake could not hear what was being said, but he could see the man shaking hands with the one Jake thought was probably the leader.

When it looked like the cowboys were going to leave the cabin, Jake quickly ducked back around the corner of the cabin. Staying in the darkness at the end of the cabin, he watched as the three cowboys mounted and started riding back the way they had come.

Concerned that he might be seen if he headed back to his horse, Jake stayed in the dark shadow at the end of the cabin. While he waited for the lights inside to go out, he thought about what he saw and what he was going to do about it. He waited for over twenty minutes after the lights went out before he snuck back to where he had left his horse.

When he got back to his horse, he swung into the saddle and slowly started moving in a large circle around behind the cabin. When he came to the edge of the draw, he could just barely make out the cattle. He could also see that part of the draw had been fenced off for a corral to keep the cattle in. Jake also noticed a man sitting on the fence next to the gate. Although he was hard to see, he could tell the man at the gate had a rifle resting across his lap.

Since Jake had a good idea what was going on, it was time for him to get out of there before he was spotted. He turned his horse and headed back the way he had come.

Being watchful, Jake rode back to his camp and went inside the tent. He got ready for bed and laid down to sleep, but sleep didn't come right away. He had too much on his mind. He knew of three cowboys who had stolen cattle. The problem was, how was he going to prove it? He had to have witnesses if he was going to take them in and charge them with rustling. He finally dozed off without a plan to solve his problem.

When morning came, he built a small fire to cook his breakfast and made a pot of coffee. As he ate, he still didn't have a plan on how he was going to prove he had seen the three cowboys drive the cattle across the Wyoming line.

By the time he finished his breakfast and had his second cup of coffee, he had come up with a plan. He put out his fire, packed up his belongings and started to head west toward the Wyoming line. He was going to use his cover as a bounty hunter to stop in at the cabin where the cowboys got paid for the cattle.

He made sure he stayed well south of the cabin so he could ride up to the cabin from the south. When he came to the top of a hill overlooking the cabin, he continued to ride down the other side toward the cabin. He was not very far from the cabin when a man stepped out on the front porch and looked toward him. The man was holding a rifle loosely in his hand.

Jake was ready for any kind of trouble. He had a small pistol behind his back, tucked in his belt. He could get it in a hurry, and it would be a surprise to anyone. He rode right up to the front of the cabin and looked down at the man with the rifle.

"Hello," Jake said.

"Hello," the man responded cautiously.

"My name's Jake Murdock. I was wondering if you might have seen this man," he said as he reached into his shirt pocket and pulled out the wanted poster.

Jake held the wanted poster out as he leaned forward in the saddle so the man could step closer and look at it. The man hesitated a moment before he stepped off the porch and reached up to take the wanted poster. He tucked the rifle under his arm, then open the folded paper. He looked at it for a moment then handed it back to Jake.

"Nope. Haven't seen anyone like that around here," the man said as he watched Jake fold the wanted poster and put it back in his pocket.

"Thanks. I guess I'll head back and see if I can pick up his trail where I lost it. That rain last night sort of wiped it out. Are there any other ranches or farms around here where he might hold up for awhile?"

"The closest ranch is about ten, eleven miles east of here. It's a pretty big spread. That wanted poster said he held up the bank in Belle Fourche. What makes you think he came this way?"

"A lawman I talked to said he was headed this way, but like I said, I lost his trail so I kept moving in the same direction. I guess he must have changed directions. Thanks for your help," Jake said as he reached up and touched the brim of his hat.

Jake turned his horses and headed east toward where the man had said there was a large ranch. He didn't look back. He simply rode away. When Jake got far enough away from the cabin and had crossed over a hill, he turned and rode north along the side of the hill. As soon as he had gone a few hundred yards from where he crossed the ridge, he stopped and swung out of the saddle. He tied his horses to a small tree in a ravine, took his field glasses out of his saddlebags and walked up the hill. When he was almost at the top, he crouched down and worked his way to the top.

As soon as he was where he could see the cabin, he knelt down and put the field glasses up to his eyes. Jake scanned the area around the cabin then watched the cabin in the hope of finding out how many men might be there.

He had only been looking at the cabin for a short time when two men came up out of the draw that ran alongside and behind the cabin. It was the same draw where the cattle had been taken. The men stepped up on the porch of the cabin and talked to the man who had been in the cabin. They all looked toward where Jake had gone.

Jake smiled to himself as he walked down the hill to the bottom of the ravine where he had left his horses. It was time for Jake to visit Mr. Stapleton at his ranch. He swung into the saddle and headed east toward the Stapleton Ranch.

It was well past noon when he rode into the ranch yard of the Stapleton Ranch. Mr. Stapleton stepped out on the front porch of the ranch house when he saw Jake riding in. He wondered what he was doing there, and if he had any news for him. Just as Jake reined up in front of the hitching rail, another man stepped out of the ranch house.

"Good afternoon. Would I be correct in assuming that you are Mr. Stapleton?"

Mr. Stapleton was a little confused by Jake's question. It suddenly occurred to him that Jake didn't want anyone to know that they knew each other.

"Yes, I'm Stapleton. This is my foreman, Tom Kaltman. Who are you and what do you want?"

"I'm Jake Murdock. I would like you to take a look at this wanted poster," Jake said as he took the wanted poster out of his shirt pocket and held it out to Mr. Stapleton. "I'd like to know if this man is here on your ranch."

Mr. Stapleton stepped closer to Jake, then reached up and took the wanted poster. He looked up at Jake, then looked back at the wanted poster. He unfolded the wanted poster and looked at it for a moment before he looked back at Jake.

"No, he doesn't work here. I don't think I've ever seen him. You look like you've come a long way. If you would like to take your horses over to the corral, they can get a drink. While they are getting a drink, you can come inside for a cup of coffee, if you like," Mr. Stapleton said.

"Thank you. Getting out of this saddle for a little while would be much appreciated."

"Do you want me to hang around?" Tom said to Mr. Stapleton while keeping an eye on Jake.

"I don't think that will be necessary. You have plenty of things to do," Mr. Stapleton said.

Mr. Stapleton watched his foreman step off the porch and walk toward the barn. As soon as he disappeared into the barn, he turned his attention to Jake.

Jake put his horses in the corral. As soon as they were drinking from the trough, he turned and walked back toward the ranch house. While walking toward the ranch house, he glanced at the foreman to see where he was going. When Jake got to the ranch house he stepped up on the porch.

"Do you think it was a good idea for you to come here?" Mr. Stapleton asked keeping his voice low.

"I don't think I have much choice. Let's go inside where we can talk where no one will see us or hear us."

"Yes. Yes, of course."

Jake followed Mr. Stapleton into the ranch house. Once inside, Jake looked around to see if there was anyone who might hear them. He didn't see anyone.

"Is it safe to talk here?" Jake asked in almost a whisper.

"Yes. Yes, of course."

"I've got some news for you that I don't think you will like. Tom, your foreman, is the leader of at least two other ranch hands who have been stealing your cattle."

"I don't believe you," he said, but didn't sound very sure.

"I watched them herd about sixty to seventy head of your cattle across the Wyoming line to a small cabin only a mile or so from the border. They ran them into a draw that had been fenced off to hold the cattle. After they had the cattle penned up, the three of them went into the cabin and were paid for the cattle."

"Do you know who the other two were?"

"No, but I would know them if I see them."

"I'll get the men to come here. See if you can pick them out."

"Okay, but you better be ready for them to try to get away. I'm sure they know that cattle rustlers are hung."

"I'll be ready," Mr. Stapleton said sharply.

Mr. Stapleton turned and walked to the door. One of the ranch hands was walking across the ranch yard from the bunkhouse toward the barn.

"Dusty," Mr. Stapleton called out.

"Yes, sir," Dusty said as he turned and walked toward Mr. Stapleton.

"I want you to tell Tom to get all the men together and come over to the ranch house."

"All the men, sir?"

"All of them who are here. He doesn't have to call in those who are watching over the cattle in the pastures. And tell him I want them here as soon as possible."

"Yes, sir," Dusty said, then headed toward the bunkhouse.

Mr. Stapleton watched as Dusty headed toward the bunkhouse. He turned around and found Jake standing in the doorway watching him. Mr. Stapleton wasn't sure what Jake was thinking. Jake was sure Mr. Stapleton didn't like the idea that some of his men were rustlers.

It didn't take long for the men to start showing up in front of the ranch house. Jake watched for the men he had seen selling Mr. Stapleton's cattle. One of the first ones to show up was Tom Kaltman. Jake got the feeling that Tom was more than a little suspicious of him. Jake had no idea what Tom might do if he was confronted with charges of rustling his boss's cattle. He could see the way Tom carried his gun, low on the hip and tied down. That didn't mean anything, but it was a clue that he might be pretty handy with a gun.

"As some of you already know, we have been having cattle rustled from here and taken to Wyoming where they are sold," Mr. Stapleton began. "We now have a pretty good idea who the rustlers are."

Two of the men standing in front of Mr. Stapleton and Jake began looking around. Tom lowered his hand closer to his gun while looking at Jake.

"Who is the man standing with you," Tom asked.

"He is Jake Murdock. For those of you who might not know why he is here, he is a bounty hunter I hired to find out who was stealing my cattle. He has already told me who the rustlers are."

Suddenly, one of the rustlers drew his gun and pointed it at Mr. Stapleton.

"You ain't hanging me for cattle rustling," the man said as he backed away.

"It won't do you any good to run, Josh. We all know you are one of them. You just gave yourself away," Mr. Stapleton said.

With the distraction caused by Josh, Tom was able to move to the corner of the ranch house and slip around behind it. From there, he ran toward the barn.

Tom thought he had gotten away, but Jake had seen him. Before Jake could make a move to catch Tom, a shot was fired and Josh doubled over and fell to the ground. When Jake turned back to see what had happened, the third man had been grabbed by the cowboys standing there. Seeing that two of the rustlers had been caught, Jake headed for the barn.

As Jake was approaching the barn door, Tom came racing out of the barn on a horse. He fired a shot at Jake as he almost ran Jake down. Jake had to jump out of the way. In doing so, he fell to the ground, Tom's shot missed Jake by only a couple of inches.

Tom quickly turned the horse and rode hard toward a row of trees. Jake stood up, took careful aim and fired. The bullet struck Tom in the back. Tom fell from the horse. Jake started running toward him.

When Jake got to Tom, he was breathing heavily. Tom looked up at Jake, but didn't move. It was easy to see that Jake's bullet had severed Tom's spine. Without a word Tom closed his eyes and took his last breath.

Mr. Stapleton walked up next to Jake and looked down at his foreman.

"He was a good foreman. What do you suppose caused him to steal my cattle?"

"Only he would know the answer to that," Jake said.

Mr. Stapleton and Jake returned to the ranch house. Once inside, Mr. Stapleton sat down at his desk. He took out some money from one of the drawers and counted out three thousand dollars. He turned around and handed it to Jake.

"You earned this," he said.

Jake took the money and tucked it inside his shirt.

"What about the men in Wyoming, and the man your men have?"

"My men will take care of them," Mr. Stapleton said. "Thanks for your help."

Jake nodded that he understood. It was not what he wanted to happen to the rustlers, but he knew they would get what the law would have dished out anyway.

His job was done there. He walked over to his horses and untied them. Once in the saddle, he turned his horse and led his packhorse away from the Stapleton Ranch. It was time to head back to Hill City.

CHAPTER SEVEN

Tracking a Killer

When Jake arrived in Hill City, his first stop was at the livery stable to put his horses up for a good rest. He had just stepped out of the saddle when he was greeted by Joe Wilcox, the blacksmith and owner of the livery stable.

"Boy, am I glad to see you," Joe said, his voice showing how excited he was that Jake had returned.

"Slow down. What's going on?"

"Some guy come inta town and shot Marshal Walker."

"What? Is he okay?"

"He's at the doc's office. He's in bad shape, but still hanging in there, so I'm told. Doc won't let no one talk to him or see him."

"Take care of my horses for me?"

"Sure thing. I get along with your horse pretty well now that he's gotten used to me."

Jake hardly waited for Joe to finish answering before he was running down the street toward the doc's office. He ran up the stairs and went into the doctor's office. The first thing he saw was Doc sitting at his desk. Jake took a quick look around the room. In the corner, on the far side of the room, was a bed. He could see Marshal Walker was lying in the bed. It looked as if he was sleeping. Jake walked up to the doctor.

"How's he doing, Doc?" Jake asked in a whisper, hoping not to disturb John.

"It's been tough, but I think he's going to make it."

"Do you know what happened?"

"The way it was told to me, four cowboys came into town and got in a fight with a couple of miners in the Golden Nugget Saloon. John ran over to the saloon to break it up and was shot just as he entered the saloon. He didn't even have his gun in his hand. He never had a chance.

"By the time things settled down, two miners lay dead on the floor, one wounded, and John laid on the boardwalk in front of the saloon with a bullet in his upper chest and one in his side. The one in his side wasn't all that bad. It didn't hit any major blood vessels, organs, or any of his ribs. It was the one in his chest that has been the problem."

"Can you describe the men who shot him?"

"I can do better than that. From what little I could find out, the one who shot John was Les Carpenter. I don't know who the rest of them were."

"I'm not familiar with him. Any idea who he is or why he was here?"

"I'm told he's a gunfighter from Abilene, Texas. Word is he's a gun-for-hire to the highest bidder."

"What's he doing around here?" Jake asked.

"I'm not real sure, but I heard he was here to do a job."

Jake thought for a moment. He wondered what job Carpenter had been hired to do.

"If he's a hired gun, any idea who he was here to kill?"

"No, but they left town as soon as they shot John. They didn't stick around long enough to make sure John was dead."

"Any idea where they were going from here?"

"No, but James at the Golden Nugget Saloon might know more about what happened. He's the one who told me what I've told you."

"Can I talk to John?"

"I'm sorry, but I don't think that's a good idea. He's resting. It's best we let him rest," Doc said with a hint of apology in his voice. "I know you are friends, but he is in pretty bad shape, and I doubt he could tell you anything right now anyway."

"I understand, Doc," Jake said sounding a little disappointed.

"What are you going to do now?"

"I going to go have a talk with James and see if he can give me any more information. Then, I'm going after them."

"You be careful. From what little I've been told, this Les Carpenter fella is as deadly as a rattlesnake."

"I've dealt with rattlesnakes before. I'll be careful, and I'll get them, too," Jake said with a strong note of anger in his voice.

Jake took a look at his friend lying on the bed for just a minute before he turned and left Doc's office. He walked down the street to the Golden Nugget Saloon. Jake walked into the saloon and found James standing behind the bar.

"James, I need to talk to you."

"Sure thing, Deputy. Let's go to the backroom," he said.

"Annie, watch the bar for a bit. I need to talk to Jake."

"Sure," Annie replied.

Jake followed James to the backroom then closed the door behind him. They walked over to a table and sat down.

"Tell me what happened to John. From what Doc told me, it was almost as if John was gunned down without a chance to defend himself."

"It sure looked that way to me. In fact, it looked like he was set up."

"What do you mean?"

"I'll start at the beginning. Day before yesterday, four men rode into town. They came in here and sat down, had a couple of drinks then left. I heard later that they visited a couple of the other saloons. We didn't see much of them until last evening. It was kind of quiet in here.

"The four of them sat down in the corner for awhile, not doing anything but talking among themselves. After a while, one of them walked over to the window and just stood there looking out. After about twenty to thirty minutes, the one looking out the window hurried back to the table where the others were sitting.

"Almost immediately, it looked to me like the one called Les motioned for the other three to start a fight with a couple of miners. As far as I could tell, the miners had been mindin' their own business. They had been here for almost an hour without any trouble.

"Any idea what the fight was about?"

"No. The three cowboys just started callin' 'um names and eggin' the miners on."

"What was this guy, Les, doing?"

"Well, he was sort of watching the cowboys a bit, but he seemed more interested in anyone who might come in and end the fightin'," James said with a confused look on his face.

"Are you sure he was just watching for someone, or was he watching for John?"

James looked at Jake for a minute while he thought about what Jake had said. The thought that Jake might be right caused him to think a little harder.

"You know, Les shot John almost as soon as he stepped in the door. John didn't even have his gun in his hand. It was almost as if this Les fella was waiting for John," James said thoughtfully.

"Ya know, as I think about it, Les seemed a bit disappointed that it was the marshal," James said.

"What do you mean?"

"Well, it was almost as if he was expecting someone else," James said as if he wasn't really sure of what he actually saw.

Jake looked at James. He wasn't sure what to make of what he had just been told. If Les had shot John by mistake, who was he really after? Since John was the only lawman in town, who else was he after. Then a thought hit Jake like a bolt of lightning. Was Les really after him?

"Do you think he might have been looking to kill me?" Jake asked.

"I never thought of that. I don't know, but as soon as they discovered they had shot the marshal, two of the others shot the miners then they got out of town. I ain't never seen anyone leave so fast as them four."

"Did they ask about me at any time? You know, like where I was or when I might be making rounds?"

"No, but now that I have a chance to think on it, I heard them mention among themselves something about a lawman. They never mentioned a name, at least not that I heard. I guess I just assumed they were talking about John. I guess they could have been talking about you. You're the only other lawman we've had in this town for the past three or four years."

Jake had never heard of Les Carpenter before. If Les was after him, what was his reason? Why would he have been hired to kill him? Jake wondered if a friend or relative of one of the men he had brought to justice might have hired Les Carpenter to kill him, but didn't know there were two lawmen in Hill City much of the time.

"What are you thinking about," James asked.

"I was just thinking. This Carpenter fella might have been hired to kill the marshal because the person who had hired Les had had some trouble with a lawman here. There's also the possibility that he was here to kill me, but didn't know that I was only a part-time lawman," Jake said as he thought about it.

"I guess that's possible, but how you going to know if they were after you?"

"That's a good question," Jake replied.

"What are you going to do?"

"I'm going to hunt down the three men who fought and killed the miners, and Les Carpenter for shooting my friend and the marshal of Hill City."

"They've got a big lead on you. It could take you all the way to Texas to catch up with them. And once you find them, you'll have four of them to deal with," James said with a concerned tone in his voice.

"I'm sure you're right, but I'll follow them into hell, if that's what it takes to get them," Jake said in anger as he stood up. "John is my friend. I will not let them get away with shooting him."

James nodded his head in response as Jake turned and walked out of the backroom of the Golden Nugget Saloon and on out the swinging doors in the front of the saloon. James followed him as far as the swinging doors. He stopped at the doors, but continued to watch Jake as he walked toward the livery stable.

It was only a few minutes before Jake walked into the livery stable. Both his horses had been well cared for by Joe. Jake took his saddle off the top rail of the stall and walked over to his horse.

"Where ya going, Jake?" Joe asked.

"I'm going after the men who shot John."

"It'll be dark in less than an hour. Your horses need some rest. Why don't you wait 'til tomorrow? You could use a little rest, too, ya know."

Jake looked at Joe for a second, then looked at his horses. He was tired and so were his horses. They needed rest as much as he did. It was time to rest and plan things out.

"You're right. I'm going to get a good meal, then get some rest. I'll leave in the morning."

"I'll have your horses ready to go first thing in the morning."

"Thanks, Joe," Jake said, then turned and walked toward Sharon's boarding house.

Jake entered the boarding house just in time for dinner. He sat down and had a good meal. When he was finished, he went up to his room, took off his boots, and got ready for bed. He laid down on the bed with his hands behind his head as he looked up at the ceiling. He thought about what he had been told by James and Doc. If they were headed back to Texas, they probably would go through Custer City and Hot Springs then head on south into the Nebraska Territory. He would head that way in the hope of picking up their trail.

With a plan set in his mind, Jake's thoughts turned to his first meeting with John when he first became a lawman, and how their friendship had grown. It wasn't long before Jake drifted off to sleep.

Jake woke and turned his head toward the window. He could see that the sky was just beginning to get light. He rolled over and sat up on the edge of the bed. His thoughts were of what he was about to do.

He got up, poured water into a bowl from a pitcher on the washstand in the corner, then washed his face and ran his hands through his hair. As soon as he was dressed, he strapped his gun belt around his waist. Jake carefully checked his gun to make sure it was ready to use before he left the room. He went downstairs to the kitchen of the boarding house where he had a good breakfast. He couldn't help but think it was going to be the best breakfast he would probably have for some time.

After breakfast, he left the boarding house and walked down the street to the livery stable. Just as he arrived, Joe was bringing his horses out of the stable. His horse was saddled and his packhorse had been packed with supplies. Jake noticed that there was a long-barreled rifle tied on the packhorse's pack frame. He walked up to his packhorse and looked at the rifle. Jake noticed it had a telescope on the barrel. He turned and looked at Joe, Joe was looking at him.

"I thought you might need a rifle that shoots a long way," Joe said with a grin. "There's a lot of open country between here and Abilene, Texas."

"Where'd you get a rifle like that?" Jake asked.

"It was my rifle during the Civil War. I was a sharpshooter during the war. Because of my bum leg, I wasn't any good in the infantry. But because I could shoot better than most of them other men when I volunteered, they made me a sharpshooter. I don't have much need for that kind of rifle any more, but thought you might could use it."

"Thank you. I'll take good care of it."

"You just get them fellas that shot John."

"I'll do my best," Jake said as he reached out and shook Joe's hand.

Jake turned and swung into the saddle. He turned his horses and started south out of town. As soon as he was out of town, he began looking for tracks of four horses headed south. It was hard to find tracks that he was sure belonged to the four men he was after.

His first stop would be Custer City where he would visit Sheriff Metcalf. Jake would see how he was doing after the shootout they had sometime ago, and talk to him about the four men.

It was mid-afternoon when Jake arrived in Custer City. He rode up to the sheriff's office and stepped out of the saddle. He looked around as he tied his horses to the hitching rail. When he turned around to go into the sheriff's office, he saw Sheriff Metcalf standing in the doorway smiling at him.

"It sure is good to see you on your feet," Jake said.

"I'm still on crutches, but I'm getting around. Charlie does most the legwork. That shot in the leg busted up my leg pretty bad, worse than Doc first thought."

"I'm glad to hear you're getting better. How much longer before you get rid of the crutches?"

"Doc thinks I should be able to get along without them in about another month or so. Come inside. What brings you down this way?" Sheriff Metcalf asked.

"I'm trying to pick up the tracks of four men. The leader is Les Carpenter from Abilene, Texas. The word is they are headed back to Texas."

"What's your interest in them?"

"They shot Marshal Walker. It was the guy by the name of Les Carpenter who shot John as he ran into the Golden Nugget Saloon to break up a fight between three cowboys and some miners. They didn't kill him, but he's in pretty bad shape. He'll probably be laid up for six months or more."

"I take it there's a reward for this Les Carpenter?" Sheriff Metcalf asked.

"There might be, but I don't know of one. This is one guy I'd be happy to hunt down for free. I didn't just work for John, he's my friend."

"I understand," Sheriff Metcalf said. "Four men road through town yesterday. They stopped off at the general store and picked up a few things, then left town. I don't think they were here for more than a couple of hours before they left."

"Can you give me some idea of what they looked like?"

"The one that seemed to be the leader was fairly tall. He was dressed in black from head to toe. This might help. He had some kind of a silver medal on his holster and wore some pretty fancy black boots. You don't see much of that stuff around here. He rode a black horse with a white blaze on its face and white sox on its front feet."

"That's good to know. What about the three with him?"

"The other three were dressed like cowboys and rode horses that were brown. One of the horses had a star shaped white marking on its face, and one had white on his chest. I didn't see any markings on the third horse.

"Two of the riders were of average size and carried Colt Peacemakers. Nothing special about those two. The third rider was tall, slim, and had a scar on his left cheek. He carried an Army Colt tied down low on his left leg. Oh, they all carried Winchester saddle rifles," Sheriff Metcalf said.

"That's more information on what they looked like than what I had so far."

"I'm afraid I can't help you with something that would make it easier for you to track them."

"What you've told me will make it a lot easier to spot them. I best be on my way. It could take me awhile to catch up with them."

"You take care of yourself. I'll send Charlie over to keep law and order in Hill City 'til either John can take care of it himself or you get back."

"I appreciate that, and I'm sure John will, too."

Jake swung into the saddle and rode out of Custer City. He headed south toward Hot Springs. If they were headed back to Abilene, there was a good chance they headed straight back which means they would go almost straight south through Hot Springs.

Jake arrived in Hot Springs shortly before dark. As he rode down the street to the hotel, he spotted Sheriff Sam Tidwell walking across the street. Jake called out to him.

"Sheriff Tidwell."

Sam stopped and looked toward Jake. He didn't recognize Jake so he put his hand over his gun, then waited for Jake to ride toward him.

"Sheriff, I'm Jake Murdock."

"Hi. I've heard of you. Looks like you're planning on a long trip," Sam said as he looked at the packhorse Jake had in tow.

"It just might be."

"How can I help you?"

"I would like to talk to you about some men who might have passed through here either early this morning or late yesterday."

"You look like you've traveled a long way. Are you going to stay the night or press on?"

"I think I will stay the night. I could use the rest, so could my horses."

"Take your horses over to the livery stable then meet me at Ruth's boarding house. You can get something to eat while we talk, and you can get a room for the night."

"That's a good idea. I'll meet you there shortly," Jake said.

Sheriff Tidwell watched Jake ride on down the street to the livery stable. He knew Jake was a bounty hunter and sometimes worked for Marshal Walker. He wondered what it was that brought Jake to Hot Springs.

As soon as Jake disappeared into the livery stable, Sheriff Tidwell walked over to Ruth's boarding house. He sat down at a table in the dining room to wait for Jake.

It didn't take Jake long to get his horses taken care of and walk to Ruth's boarding house. When he walked in the door, he was met by a very nice looking woman. She was a few years older than Jake and had a pleasant smile.

"Are you Mr. Murdock?" she asked.

"Yes."

"Sheriff Tidwell is waiting for you in the dining room. This way," she said as she turned and walked into the dining room.

"Did you get your horses taken care of?" Sheriff Tidwell asked as Jake entered the dining room.

"I did. They are getting something to eat?" Jake said as he pulled out a chair and sat down at the table.

"Good. Ruth, could we get something to eat. I'm sure my friend is rather hungry."

"I'll have something for him in a few minutes. In the meantime, I'll get you gentlemen some coffee."

"Thank you, Ruth." Sheriff Tidwell said then turned and looked at Jake. "You want to tell me what your interest is in the men you think might have passed through my town?"

"First of all, you might like to know that the men I'm after apparently ambushed Marshal Walker. They didn't kill him, but he was shot up pretty bad."

"I know Marshal Walker. He's a good man."

Jake went on to tell Sheriff Tidwell what had happened. Tidwell took a great deal of interest in what Jake had to say. Tidwell gave Jake a description of the four men. It matched what Jake had learned from Sheriff Metcalf in Custer City.

"Do you have any idea why they would come all the way up here to kill him?"

"No. From what I have heard, Les Carpenter is a hired gun. I don't think he was hired to kill John. I think he was hired to kill me."

"What gives you that idea?"

"They apparently didn't know what I look like. John is about my height and weight, and he has brown hair like me. They might not know how old the guy they were after was. All they seemed to know was the person they were hired to kill was a lawman in Hill City. I don't think they realized that Hill City had two lawmen, at least part of the time," Jake explained.

"Where were you when John was shot?"

"I was on my way back from Belle Fourche where I was hired to look for some cattle rustlers. I got them and was on my way back to Hill City when John was ambushed. If I had returned a day earlier, they might have gotten the right person," Jake said.

"I take it from what you say that you're not sure that you were the one they were supposed to ambush. Maybe it was John they intended to kill," Tidwell said.

"You might be right. I'm not sure, but just from what James, the barkeeper at the Golden Nugget Saloon, told me, I got the feeling the shooter wasn't sure himself."

Tidwell thought for a minute before he said, "There were four men who left town together this morning. From your description, it's likely they were the ones you are looking for. They didn't seem to be in any hurry."

"Then they don't know someone is after them," Jake said thoughtfully. "Maybe they thought they had finished the job they were hired to do."

"It certainly didn't appear that they had any idea they were being followed."

"Good. If they don't think anyone is after them, they won't be traveling hard and fast."

Just then, Ruth came into the dining room with two large plates. Each plate had a large steak and a good helping of fried potatoes. She set the plates on the table.

"Is there anything else I can get you?"

"No, I don't think so. Thanks, Ruth," Sam said.

"Good. Be sure to leave room for fresh baked apple pie. Enjoy, gentlemen," she said then left the room.

Jake and Sam began to eat. It was some time before either of them talked again. Sam spoke first.

"Do you have any idea who hired this Les Carpenter?"

"No idea," Jake said. "I'm hoping to catch a least one of them alive so I can find out."

"These are hard men. They won't give up that kind of information easily."

"I'm sure you're right. If I don't find out, I will have to watch my back until I find out who wants me dead."

Sam just nodded his head in agreement while he took another bite of his steak. He didn't say anything more for awhile, but it was clear that he was thinking.

"Jake, I can't go with you, but maybe I can help you. If they are returning to Texas, they will have to head into the Nebraska Territory. There's a lot of open ground between here and the rougher country of Pine Ridge. Once they get across the ridge, its wide open and fairly flat all the way south into northern Texas.

"In the open ground before you get to the ridge, it would be easy for them to spot you from some distance. You'll need to be very careful."

"I know, but I have an advantage," Jake said with a grin.

"How so?"

"I have field glasses to see them before I get very close, and a long range rifle with a scope on it. As far as I know, they have only saddle rifles and side arms."

"You still have to see them first," Sam reminded him.

"I'm hoping to find their tracks. It shouldn't be too hard once I get out on the prairie. I just have to find four shod horses moving south together."

"Good luck with that," Sam said with a grin.

As soon as they finished eating, they said goodnight. Sam left the boarding house while Jake went to his room. It didn't take Jake long to get ready for bed. Once he was in bed, he thought about what Sam had told him. He knew it was not going to be easy, but Jake had learned to be careful, and to keep his eyes open for danger. It wasn't long before Jake drifted off to sleep.

CHAPTER EIGHT

The Chase in On

Jake woke early. He was out of bed, dressed and having breakfast before the sun came up. As soon as he finished eating, he gathered his belongings and walked down the street to the livery stable. It didn't take him long to have his horses ready to go. He rode out of Hot Springs just as the sun was coming up over the hills to the east.

The road Jake was traveling would take him south toward Louis Chartron's Trading Post on Chadron Creek in the Nebraska Territory. If he didn't catch up with Les Carpenter soon, he would continue south toward Sidney.

The road south toward Chadron Creek wound its way along a shallow river for a short distance and then out onto the open prairie with its rolling hills and tall grass, but very few trees. Once out in the open, Jake would have to be very careful. Although the prairie looked to be almost flat, there were many places where the land dipped into ravines and gullies, some of them deep enough to hide a man on a horse.

Many of the ravines and gullies that had creeks in them, also had trees along their banks. They made good places for those crossing the prairie to settle in for the night, get out of the winds that often blew across the open prairie as well as provide some shelter from the hot sun during the long hot summer days. Those same ravines and gullies would also make good places where Jake could be ambushed, if Les Carpenter and his men saw him first.

Time passed slowly as Jake followed the dirt road as it wound its way out of Hot Springs and out of the Black Hills. The gently rolling hills of the prairie stretched out over the land as far as the eye could see. It was late afternoon by the time Jake was headed out onto the prairie.

Once out of the Black Hills, Jake knew that it was going to be harder to follow the four men with so few places to hide. If they were watching to see if anyone was following them, they might see him before he saw them. If that happened, they could find a place to ambush him. Jake would have to be watchful at all times.

On the third day out from Hot Springs, Jake reached the wooded ridge known as Pine Ridge because of the pine trees that covered most of the ridge. Jake slowed down in an effort to make it hard to be seen by those he was following. He carefully left the road that wound its way to the top of the ridge. He moved slowly among the trees in an effort not to be seen.

Once Jake reached the top of the ridge and could see what was on the other side, Jake moved over to the road again. He reined up his horse and stepped out of the saddle to check for the tracks of the men he was following. All he could see were the tracks of several horses and the wheel ruts caused by the stagecoaches and freight wagons that used the road from Sidney in the Nebraska Territory to Hot Springs, Custer City and Deadwood in the northern Black Hills. The freshest tracks, and the tracks that were on top of the others, were of four horses headed south.

Since all the rest of the tracks were either headed north or were old, he was sure he was on the right trail. Jake carefully studied the tracks made by the four horses. He wanted to be able to recognize the tracks even among other tracks.

Once he was sure he would be able to recognize the tracks, he stood up, removed his field glasses from his saddlebags and scanned the prairie that laid out before him. When he didn't see anything of interest to him, he got back in the saddle. He continued down off the ridge. When he got down off the ridge to where the prairie flattened out a little, all he could see was wide open spaces, with rolling hills, a blue sky with only a few thin high clouds and a few antelope off to the west.

Jake continued to follow the tracks until mid-afternoon. He noticed a hill off to the east of the trail. It was not a very high hill, but was higher than anything nearby. He rode up the nearby hill. When he was close to the top of the hill, Jake reined up and stepped out of the saddle. He stood next to his horse and reached in his saddlebags. He took his field glasses from his saddlebags, then walked toward the top of the hill until he could just see over the top and out onto the prairie below. He put his field glasses up to his eyes and carefully scanned the prairie to the south and west.

As he slowly moved the field glasses across the prairie, he suddenly stopped. There was something moving south of his location. Jake studied the area where he saw the movement. It took him a few minutes, but whatever it was he had seen had stopped moving. It wasn't until they started moving again that he could see there were four men on horseback riding south. It didn't look like they were moving very fast. In fact, it looked like they were just walking their horses. The tracks he had seen just before he rode up the hill indicated that the four horses were not in any hurry.

Jake watched them for several minutes while thinking about what he should do. It was open country. To stay out of sight, he would have to go around some of the hills which could cause him to have to travel almost twice as far. That could make it more difficult to catch up to them.

There was one thing he could do. If he remembered correctly, there was an almost full moon tonight and for the next couple of nights. He could gain ground on them if he stayed back about the same distance from them he was currently at during the day, then move closer after dark. He could hide behind the hills during the day. Within a couple of days, he should be close enough to identify them.

Jake swung into the saddle, then nudged his horses along. Every once in awhile he would stop and look at them to make sure they were still moving. He had kept an eye on them using his field glasses. Without the field glasses, he could not see them well enough to tell if it was men on horses or some large animals. Jake stayed at about the same distance from them as they continued to move south.

It was getting close to sunset when he noticed they had stopped. Jake rode a little closer to them before he stopped and stepped out of the saddle. He stood next to his horse as he watched the four men. It quickly became clear that they were stopping for the night. The place they had picked to camp was in a small grove of trees. For the trees to even be there, it had to be a ravine where water would collect when it rained, or there was a small stream or spring in the bottom of it.

Jake quickly scanned the area. He could see a hill that looked to be about four hundred yards, maybe a little further to the east of where they were setting up camp. Jake glanced at the rifle with the scope on his packhorse and began to smile. If he could get to the top of that hill without being seen, he would be in easy range with the sharpshooter's rifle. Jake sat down next to his horses to wait for it to get dark enough that he could not be seen.

As soon as it was dark enough, Jake stood up, took the reins of his horses and moved to the hill that was only about four hundred yards from where the campfire was located in among the trees. He found a place near the top of the hill where he could see the four men. It looked as if they had finished fixing dinner and were getting ready to eat.

Jake laid down in the grass and watched them for a few minutes. He carefully picked out his target. Through the scope, he could identify the four men. From what information he had obtained from the barkeeper, the one dressed all in black was Les Carpenter. This was his chance to reduce the number of men he would have to face. He took careful aim at one of the men and slowly pulled the trigger.

Les Carpenter rode up to the grove of trees with the other three riders following him. He stepped out of his saddle and looked around. He didn't see anything that should cause them harm. In fact, it looked like a place that would be comfortable, as well as safe, for the night.

"I think this is a good place to spend the night," Les said as he looked over the small grove of trees.

"Looks good to me," Chester said.

"Me, too," Mark added.

The fourth member of the group, Jess, didn't say a word. He was busy looking around, plus he was unable to talk. He had lost his ability to talk due to an encounter with an Indian when he was a ten-year-old boy. The Indian had cut out his tongue because he talked too much. He had later escaped from the Indians; and after about ten years, he joined up with Les Carpenter and his men.

When Chester looked at Jess, he wondered what he was looking at. He walked over to Jess then looked in the direction Jess was looking.

"You see something, Jess?

Jess pointed to his eye then pointed at the hill where he had seen something move.

"What did you see?"

"What's going on?" Les called out to Chester when he saw the two of them looking north toward a hill.

"Jess thinks he saw something up on that hill," Chester answered as he pointed toward the hill.

Les looked at the hill but didn't see anything except two dark spots way up close to the top of the hill.

"All I see is a couple of animals on the hillside. What does he think it is?"

"He's not sure. All he saw was something move near the top of the hill."

"It's probably a couple of buffalo. We've seen a few of them out here. In fact, we saw several just yesterday," Les said then turned and walked back to where he had left his horse.

Since Jess didn't know himself what he saw, he turned and walked back to where they were setting up camp for the night.

Nothing more was said about what Jess thought he saw. Jess gathered wood for the fire while Chester laid out the bedrolls. Mark built a fire and began fixing dinner. By the time dinner was ready, it was almost dark and they could no longer see the animals near the top of the hill. While Mark did most of the cooking, Jess sat back away from the fire. He continued to watch off to the north. Keeping the fire at his back, he could see a little better in the dark than those who stayed close to the fire.

"Jess, dinner's ready," Mark said.

Jess turned and walked over to the fire. Mark handed him a plate with his dinner on it. Jess turned and went back to where he had been sitting while watching the hills. He had just sat down when a bullet struck him in the chest. It was quickly followed by the bang of a rifle shot.

Chester and Mark dove for cover while Les Carpenter just stood there looking at Jess.

"Get down, Les," Chester yelled.

Les turned and looked at Chester as if he couldn't believe what had just happened. He just started to duck behind one of the trees when a second shot hit a rock sending sharp bits of rock flying all over. Since the bullet hit close to Les's knee, several pieces of the rock cut into his leg causing him to fall and grab his leg.

Mark ran to Les's aid while Chester grabbed the coffee pot and splashed coffee over the fire. The fire hissed and the flames went out throwing the area into darkness. With nothing left of the fire but a few coals, they could no longer be seen by the shooter.

"How bad are you hurt?" Mark asked.

"How the hell do I know? I can't see in the dark," Les said sharply while holding his leg.

"Can you walk?"

"Yeah."

"Come on. I'll help you to the other side where we can get some moonlight on you."

Mark helped Les to the other side of the small grove of trees. Once on the other side, they crawled out into the moonlight. Mark got a pretty good look at the wounds in Les's leg. None of them were very serious.

"I'll clean them up and bandage them. Your leg will be a little uncomfortable, but should heal okay."

"Did any of you see where the shots came from?" Les asked.

"Chester thought he saw a flash of light come from that hill east of us."

"Was it where Jess thought he saw something?" Les asked.

"No. It came from the hill just to the east of here." Mark said.

"That's too far for anyone to shoot and expect to hit anything," Les said sharply.

"Not if he has one of them rifles like them Yankee sharpshooters used during the Civil War."

"That's got to be four hundred yards. No one can hit a man from that distance."

Them Yankee sharpshooters could hit someone they could hardly see. I saw one of those guys hit a man at almost four hundred yards. I could hardly see the man he shot at, but he got him. The rifles them Yanks used had telescopes on 'um," Chester said.

"You mean we have someone out there who can stay out of range of our rifles and still be able to pick us off, one at a time?" Les asked, the fear of that idea clearly showing on his face.

"Yes. He can pick us off, one at a time," Mark said.

"Is there anything we can do about it?" Les asked.

"Chester is going to try and sneak around and get behind him. If he can get away from here without being seen, he stands a good chance of getting this guy," Mark said.

Mark looked up just in time to see Chester head down the ravine with a rifle in his hand. Mark had no idea if Chester could find the shooter in the dark, but it was probably their only chance.

Chester worked his way along the ravine toward the south. Knowing that the shooter was to the east of the grove, he decided to work his way around a hill located just a little east of them. He would work his way around the base of the hill and come up on the shooter from the east.

Jake had seen the first man fall from the first shot he took. He saw Les Carpenter duck just as he pulled the trigger. Jake had no idea if he had hit him, or if he had ducked in time. The last thing he saw was one of the men splashing coffee on the fire, putting the fire out. With the fire out, Jake could not see what was going on in the grove. The leaves of the trees blocked out most of the moonlight, putting almost the entire grove in darkness.

It was time for Jake to think about what they might do. He carefully watched the grove through his field glasses. He could not see any movement, and it was quiet.

Jake looked up at the sky. It was a quiet night without any breeze to cause the grass to move and make its whispery noise from the grasses rubbing together. That was good for him. It would prevent anyone from sneaking up on him. He turned and looked at his horses. They were standing only fifteen or sixteen feet from him and looked as if they were sleeping.

As Jake turned around to crawl off the top of the hill, both of the horses turned and looked at him. It was clear that almost any sound would wake them. He smiled to himself, then crawled off the top of the hill and closer to his horses. Jake noticed that as soon as he settled down and stopped moving, the horses relaxed and went back to sleep. Jake laid down in the grass several feet from the horses in the hope of getting at least an hour or two of rest.

Jake didn't know how long he had slept, but he was awakened by the sound of one of the horses snorting. He turned and looked at the horses while silently drawing his pistol for his holster.

The horses were looking off to the east. They had their heads up and ears pointed. They had heard something.

It was only a matter of a minute or so before Jake saw the shadowy figure of a man in the waning minutes of moonlight. The man was moving slowly and quietly toward where Jake was kneeling with his gun pointed at the man. The man suddenly realized that he had been seen and quickly raised his rifle, but he was too slow. Jake fired one shot at the man. As the man doubled over, he pulled the trigger. The man's shot went into the ground only a foot of so to Jake's left.

Holding his gun on the man lying on the ground, he moved close to him. The man was lying face down in the grass. Jake knelt down, picked up the man's rifle then took the holster and pistol from the man. He turned the man over. It was clear that he was dead.

Jake turned to see where his horses had gone. He discovered that they had moved off only a few yards. They were standing there looking at him. Jake quickly decided it was time to move to a different location.

He added the guns from the man he had just killed to the packs. Jake put the packs on his packhorse, then saddled his riding horse. He took hold of their reins and began leading them east. Jake walked east for a little ways then turned south. He moved along until he was sure that he was south of the grove. He crossed a shallow ravine and moved west until he was behind a low hill a little south of the grove.

Jake hobbled his horses just down off the top of the hill so they were out of sight of anyone in the grove. He then moved up to the top of the hill and looked down at the grove from the south of it. From his new position, he could see the shallow ravine as it wound its way south and west of the grove.

Jake studied the area as best he could in what little moonlight there was as the moon started down over the horizon. His thoughts turned to what the two remaining men might do. He thought that the two remaining men might try to escape using the ravine, or might try to make a run for it to the south; thinking that he was still a little north and east of them.

Since he was closer to the grove, he decided to use his Henry repeater rifle instead of the sharpshooter's rifle. He could shoot faster with the Henry, and he didn't really need a long-range rifle from his current position as he was only about a hundred to a hundred and fifty yards away, at the most.

The only thing Jake knew about the men was they had ambushed his friend and one of them was a gunfighter; but he figured they would make a break for it as soon as it was light enough to see the ground, or they would stay and try to fight him. He was betting on them trying to run.

It also crossed his mind that the gunfighter might want to stay and fight. If Les decided to run and anyone found out about it, his reputation as a gunfighter would be lost.

One look at the sky showed Jake that it would start getting light in the eastern sky, but it would be awhile before he would be able to see anything clearly. He should get in a position where he was ready for a fight no matter what they decided to do. Jake looked around for the perfect place for him to watch the grove of trees. Off to his left, there were what looked like some rocks protruding from the ground. It looked like the perfect place for him to see anyone who might decide to make a run for it. He would be able to see almost any movement around the grove, including if they tried to go back north.

After looking at the rock formation, he decided to take the sharpshooter's rifle with him. He gathered up what he would need, then walked to the rock formation. He found it would provide him with good cover to set up in among the rocks. Jake noticed that he held the high ground. Once in position and his guns were ready to use, there was nothing for him to do but wait.

When the sky had gotten light enough that it started to show more of the land, Jake could hear the sounds of horses. It was coming from inside the grove of trees. Using his field glasses, he scanned the grove. He could see the two men moving around in among the trees, but couldn't see who they were or what they were doing. He got the idea that they were putting saddles on their horses, which meant they were planning to make a run for it. Jake sat up and got ready.

All of a sudden there were two horses running out of the grove, but they were headed north. Jake immediately saw that there were no riders on the horses. It apparently was intended as a diversion in the hope of giving Les and his partner a bit of a head start.

Within seconds, two horses with riders came rushing out of the grove of trees. One headed straight south, while the other rider turned and rode west toward the ravine that ran generally southwest, but it had a short section that ran almost straight south.

Jake quickly decided to take the one coming almost straight at him. He took careful aim at the rider coming toward him. The rider saw Jake at the last second. He swung his horse around and started to gallop back toward the grove of trees. Jake took a quick shot at the rider as he raced for cover in the trees. Jake's bullet hit the man in the back. He was about to take a second shot when the rider fell off the horse. He quickly realized it was not Les Carpenter he had shot.

Jake quickly turned and took two shots at Les as he rode toward the ravine. The first shot missed, but the second shot hit the horse causing it to fall taking Les with it. Jake could see Les jump up and run toward the ravine. He took another shot at Les just as he dove into the ravine, but missed him.

Jake's location in the rocks put him about a hundred yards away and slightly uphill from the ravine. There was only a short section of the ravine that would provide Les cover. It was where the ravine made sort of a switchback. The rest of the ravine was open with no place that would provide protection. Jake could see both parts of the ravine on either side of the switchback from his position on the hill.

The shooting stopped almost as quickly as it had begun, but it wasn't over. Les was hunkered down against the side of the ravine. He knew that whoever it was shooting at him had a long-range rifle, and also had the advantage of the higher ground. Although it was a cool morning, Les was sweating. He knew if he stuck his head up to shoot at whoever it was in the rocks on the hill, he'd make himself an easy target.

The dust had settled and quiet had returned to the prairie. The early morning air was cool, but with the bright sun coming over the hill to the east it would not be long before it would get very hot.

Jake kept a close eye on the ravine where Les had taken cover. It looked like it would be a standoff for awhile. Although Jake was in range for a rifle, it looked like Les had failed to take his rifle with him when his horse fell causing Les to have to scrambled into the ravine before Jake shot him.

One look at the sky and Jake knew that it was going to get very hot in that ravine, and in a very short time. Les was wearing black from head to toe, he had lost his hat when his horse was shot out from under him, and there was no water in the shallow ravine.

Jake also knew that it would get hot for him, too. The difference was he had a hat, lighter colored clothes, and most important of all, he had a canteen of water. He also had a long-range rifle that could be used to make Les even more uncomfortable.

The area that provided cover for Les was less than fifteen feet along the edge of the ravine. Jake picked up the sharpshooter's rifle, took careful aim at the ground at the edge of the ravine then fired. The bullet, being a large caliber, struck the ground at the edge of the ravine, sending dirt and small stones into the ravine.

Les suddenly found himself covered with dirt. The fact that the shot hit the ravine just above his head caused him to dive to the bottom of the ravine. It wasn't but a minute or so when there was a second shot that hit the edge of the ravine and rained more dirt down on him. He tried to crawl away, but there was no place to go where he couldn't be seen.

Les thought about making a run for it, but was discouraged from that idea when a third shot hit the top of the ravine. The bullet took a large chunk of dirt out of the edge of the ravine, then slammed into the opposite side of the ravine.

"Are you ready to give it up and walk out of that ravine with your hands up?" Jake yelled out.

Jake waited for an answer. He got his answer when Les suddenly popped up and fired three quick rounds at the rocks, then ducked back down. None of the bullets came anywhere close to Jake. It was clear that Les' pistol was not much good at the distance between them.

Jake let out a sigh, then raised the sharpshooter's rifle up. He rested it on a rock then squeezed the trigger. He fired three rounds from the rifle before he stopped. In those three shots, he took a good bit of dirt off the edge of the ravine.

Les ducked down after his shots and was soon getting chunks of dirt coming off the edge of the ravine that rained down on him. The return fire from Jake proved to be very effective. Les laid in the bottom of the ravine with his hands trying to protect his head from the dirt that rained down on him.

Jake waited to see if Les was going to give it up. After waiting for a few minutes, he thought he would fire a few more shots at the ravine. He was about to fire the next shot when he noticed Les had his hands in the air.

"Climb out of the ravine and walk toward me. I suggest you drop any weapons you might have where I can see them. If I see so much as a knife, I'll shoot you where you stand," Jake called out.

As soon as Les was standing above the ravine, he took off his holster and dropped it on the ground. With his hands in the air, he slowly walked toward Jake. He quickly noticed that Jake was not leaving the cover of the rocks.

Jake watched every move Les made. It wasn't until Les was only about fifty feet away before Jake said anything.

"Stop right there," Jake ordered.

Les stopped. He wasn't sure what Jake had in mind.

"Put your hands on your head and slowly turn all the way around."

Les did as he was told. Once he had turned completely around, he looked at Jake. Jake was still in among the rocks.

"Lay down on the ground, face down, with your legs spread and your arms out to your sides. If you make even the slightest move from that position, I'll shoot you right where you lay."

As soon as Les had done what he was told, Jake leaned his rifle up against a rock and drew his pistol. He walked up to Les, then knelt down, putting his knee in the middle of Les's back. He holstered his pistol, then pulled Les's hands behind his back. He tied his hands together using a pig-n-string, a short piece of rope normally used to tie cattle's feet together before branding the animal. It also worked very well when tying a person's hands behind his back.

Once he was tied, Jake pulled him to his feet and walked him over to Jake's horse. He took a rope off the saddle then tied one end to Les' hands.

"What now?" Les asked.

"We're going to walk back to that grove of trees," Jake said as he took hold of the reins to his horse.

"What are you going to do there?"

Jake didn't answer him. He just shoved him toward the trees. Les was less than cooperative. He had to be motivated to keep moving. It seemed to Jake that the closer they got to the grove of trees, the less he wanted to go.

"You can't hang me without a trial," Les said as Jake shoved him along.

Jake did not respond.

Once they were in the trees, Jake picked out a tree that looked like a good place to secure Les. He walked him up to the tree then turned him around and backed him up against the tree.

Les looked at him for a moment. Jake took the other end of the rope and threw it over a branch above Les's head. He then pulled it up tight causing Les to bend over at the waist as his hands rose up behind his back. Jake tied the end of the rope to the tree where Les would not be able to reach it.

"Don't go away," Jake said.

Jake walked over to his horse and swung into the saddle then rode to where Les's horse had fallen. The horse was dead. He then rode over the hills and retrieved his packhorse. While he was there, he buried the man he had killed during the night, then took his packhorse to the grove of trees.

Jake buried the other men he had killed, then rounded up the remaining horses. It didn't take him long to find the horses. He took the horses back to the grove of trees. He took a minute to check on Les as he tied the horses to a nearby tree. Once the horses were secure, and the dead were buried, it was time to head back to Hill City.

"You have to let me loose. Being tied like this is very painful," Les said.

"Being shot in the chest is very painful, too. I'm interested in knowing something. Was Marshal Walker the person you were supposed to kill in Hill City?"

"You'll never know," Les said, but there was fear in his eyes.

"I would like to know who hired you to kill him."

"Nobody."

"I think that was the right answer. Nobody hired you to kill him. I think you were hired to kill me."

Les looked at him. For the first time, fear showed on his face.

"What are you talking about?" Les said.

"You were to kill the law officer in Hill City. The problem for you was, you didn't know there were two law officers in Hill City. You shot the wrong one. You shot Marshal Walker by mistake. By the way, when I left Hill City to come after you, he was still very much alive."

Les looked at Jake as if he had seen a ghost, a ghost that was going to kill him.

"I'm going to take you back to Hill City where you will be tried by a circuit court judge and hung by Marshal Walker."

Les had nothing more to say. His mind was too busy trying to figure out how he was going to escape.

"It's time to start back," Jake said.

Jake brought one of the horses up close to the tree, untied Les from the tree and put him on the horse. He then took the rope he had used to tie Les to the tree and tied his feet together under the horse's belly then brought the rope up and looped it around Les's chest and tied the end to the saddle horn.

"I wouldn't try to get away. You would starve to death if you escape. I will be the one who feeds you and gives you water. If you do escape, I wonder who will give out first, you or the horse. Either way, you lose."

With that said, Jake tied the reins of the horse Les was on to his packhorse. He tied the other horses in line behind the packhorse. He then swung into the saddle of his horse and nudged the horses north.

It took Jake six days to get back to Hill City. Les was much easier to get along with by the time they got to Hill City. The only time he was out of the saddle was when they stopped for the night. When they passed through Hot Springs and Custer City, Jake would have him locked up for the night in the local jail.

When they arrived back in Hill City, Jake rode up to the jail and tied his horse to the hitching rail. He tied up the horse Les had been tied on, then got Les off the horse and marched him into the jail where he locked him up. He checked in with Charlie, the young man who had been helping out while John was laid up.

As soon as Les was secure in jail and Charlie was there to keep an eye on Les, Jake took the horses to the livery stable and asked Joe to take care of them. Jake then walked back to the jail and checked in with Charlie.

Since all was secure at the jail and Jake was sure that Les was not going any place, he walked down the street to Doc's office. He walked in and found John was sitting up. He was still a long way from returning to the duties of the town marshal. They talked for a little while, then Jake left and went to the boarding house to get a good meal. Jake returned to the jail and took over the job of being the town marshal which allowed Charlie to return to Custer City.

The next week, the circuit court judge came to town. They had a trial. Les Carpenter was found guilty of trying to kill the marshal and was hung the next day.

As temporary marshal, Jake had the duty of hanging Les Carpenter since John had not recovered enough to get out of Doc's office. Les never did tell Jake who had hired him, or if he had really been hired to kill him.

Jake stayed on as marshal through the winter. When John was feeling like it, he would make rounds of the town with Jake. By spring, John had almost completely recovered from his wounds. Jake and John still made rounds of the town together. By late spring, John had recovered and was ready to take back the full duties of Town Marshal.

There had been a reward for the four men who had tried to kill the marshal. Jake collected it and put it in the bank. He continued to work with John.

CHAPTER NINE

Hill City Bank Robbed

It had been a long winter in Hill City, but the spring had come with a good mix of rain and sunshine. The wild flowers covered a lot of the ground, and the grass grew thick and green. The only problem seemed to be when it rained the streets would turn to mud making it difficult for people to cross the street without getting mud all over themselves and tracking it into the stores. The muddy streets also made it hard for the large freight wagons to move up and down the streets.

It was early May when there was an unusually heavy downpour that turned the streets of Hill City into a thick sticky mud. It was on that day that a small group of men rode into town.

It was about two-thirty in the afternoon when the sky cleared and the sun was shining once again. Jake was walking along the boardwalk about three blocks from the bank when he noticed five men riding along the main street. Their horses were covered with mud indicating that they had been ridden hard and probably for some distance. He turned and watched the five men.

The men rode slowly along the street until they came to the bank. They stopped in front of the bank and looked around for a minute before one of the riders got off his horse. He went into the bank while the others sat on their horses and looked over the town.

Jake stood on the boardwalk and leaned against a post while he watched the five men. He had no reason to be suspicious of them, but he reached down drew his gun up, then set it back down lightly in his holster making it ready for a smooth draw in case he needed it quickly. The only things that had caught Jake's attention were the facts that the five men were well armed, and they looked around as if sizing up the town.

They had only been in front of the bank for a short time, maybe five minutes, when the rider who had entered the bank came out. He looked up at the others and talked to those who had been sitting on their horses. After what appeared to be a short conversation among the five men, the rider mounted his horse and the five of them rode off toward the livery stable.

Curious about what was going on, Jake walked down the street to the bank. When he arrived at the bank, he looked toward the livery stable. The men were talking to the blacksmith in front of his shop and livery stable.

Jake turned and walked into the bank. The teller was busy with a customer so he stood back and watched.

As soon as the woman customer finished her business, she turned to leave. She smiled at Jake when he reached up and touched the brim of his hat. When she had walked passed him, Jake turned and stepped up to the teller's window.

"Good afternoon, Deputy. What can I do for you today?"

"I'd like a little information. Can you tell me anything about the man who just left here? What was his name?"

"He said he is Jacob Runyon, and he is from Kansas."

"Did he tell you what he was doing here?"

"No, not really, but he opened an account and left five hundred dollars with us."

"Did he give you any idea what he planned to do?" Jake asked.

"He said he just wanted to leave it here for safe keeping. He plans to pick it up first thing in the morning and go on to Belle Fourche. Since he was dressed like a cowboy and going to Belle Fourche, I assume that he is going to the livestock pens there to buy some cattle."

"Thanks," Jake said then started to turn around to leave when the teller interrupted him.

"Is there something wrong?" the teller asked his face showing his concern.

"Not that I know of," Jake said with a smile, then turned and walked out of the bank.

Jake stepped out on the boardwalk and looked toward the livery stable. The five men were just coming out of the stable. Jake watched them as they walked to the boardwalk and stepped up on it. They stomped most of the mud off their boots then started walking along the boardwalk. Since they were walking toward him, Jake just stood there and watched them.

As the men approached him, Jake got a good look at them. He was pretty sure he had never seen them before. The one who seemed to be the leader smiled at Jake as he drew close.

"Howdy, Marshal," the man said as he walked by.

"Good afternoon, gentlemen," Jake replied.

Jake turned and watched the five men as they walked down the boardwalk toward the Silver Dollar Saloon. As soon as they were in the saloon, Jake turned and walked back to the marshal's office. When he entered the office, he found John sitting at his desk reading the newspaper.

"All quiet out there?" John asked looking over the top of the newspaper.

"I think so," Jake replied as he looked off into space.

"Something on your mind? You look concerned about something."

"I got a feeling that the five riders who came into town a little bit ago are intending to do something, but I'm not sure what." Jake said thoughtfully.

"What gives you that idea?"

"I can't put my finger on it, but there's something about them that just doesn't add up."

"Well, if you figure it out, let me in on it," John said then went back to reading his newspaper.

Jake nodded, then turned and looked out the window. He wasn't looking at anything in particular, just looking while he thought about what he had seen. There was something about the five riders that didn't set well with him. He replayed in his mind what he had seen from the time he first saw them, up to the time they went into the Silver Dollar Saloon.

Suddenly, it hit him. "John, I don't think those men are cowboys," Jake said.

"What makes you think that?" John said as he looked over the top of his newspaper.

"Not one of the men who rode into town had a rope on his saddle. No cowboy I have ever met, or seen, would be without a rope on his saddle, especially if they were planning on moving cattle. It is as much a part of a cowboy as his hat."

John put down his newspaper and looked at Jake.

"What do you think they are up to?"

"I'd be willing to bet that the visit to the bank was to see how it was laid out, and what kind of protection it had. The one who went inside was checking it out to find out what kind of problems they might have robbing it. The others were looking over the town to figure out the quickest way out of town with the least amount of danger to themselves."

"Are you sure?"

"No, but I'd be willing to bet on it."

"Any idea when they might hit the bank?"

"Yeah. My best guess would be when the bank opens first thing in the morning."

"Why then?"

"There would be fewer people on the street, fewer people in the bank and the bank wouldn't be expecting any problems so early in the morning."

"Why wouldn't they hit it tonight after the town quiets down and everyone has turned in?"

"They might, but I got the feeling they won't. They took their horses over to the livery stable. They probably want them well fed, rubbed down and ready for a long hard ride in the morning. The bank opens about a half hour after Joe opens the livery stable. They probably know that," Jake said then thought of something else.

"They might not hit the bank until morning because if they try to take the bank after the town quiets down, they would have to deal with that big safe in the bank. It would be easier if they hit in the morning right after it opens and the safe is open. That's why they deposited five hundred dollars in the bank for safe keeping until morning. It was to make sure the safe would be opened when they went in. The teller would have to open the safe to get the man's money out for him"

"You have a point there. You got a plan to stop them?" John asked.

"Yeah, I think I have."

"Okay. Let's hear it," John said as he leaned forward, and listened to Jake's plan.

"The town is pretty quiet tonight. The weather has kept most of the usual trouble makers out of town and at home. I'll make rounds now, then go get some rest. You make rounds like you normally do before you turn in. I'll get up while the town is dark and no one is on the streets," Jake said.

"Okay. So far, so good."

"I'll keep an eye on the bank and find a place to hide near the bank. You get up at sunrise and move up to the second floor of the Red Garter Saloon right across the street from the bank. I'll be in position alongside the bank before it opens," Jake explained.

"Okay, but what happens if you're wrong and they simply withdraw their money and leave? In other words, what do we do if you're wrong?"

"Nothing. We don't do anything if that happens. We won't know if they are here to rob the bank until they rob it," Jake said with a grin. "But we'll be ready for them if they do. If nothing happens, all it will cost us is a couple of hours of sleep."

"Good thinking. I like your plan, but I think should you go get some rest. I'll go make my rounds now and again in a couple of hours. When things are quiet in town, I'll go over to the Red Garter Saloon and sack out for the night. I'll make sure I have a room on the second floor where I can look down on the bank. I'll get up before the livery stable opens. That way if things get going early, I'll be right in front of the bank and ready for it," John said.

"That's good. I'll figure on being up about the same time. I'll be in a good position so I can block their escape. If they try to rob the bank before I get there, fire a shot and I'll come running," Jake said.

"Okay. Go get some rest. It could prove to be a long night."

Jake nodded, then turned and walked out of the marshal's office. He walked down the street to Sharon's boarding house. He had his dinner then went directly to his room on the second floor in the front. He opened the window a little so he could hear if John called for him. Jake laid his gun on the table next to his bed, then laid down on his bed without taking his clothes off. He closed his eyes and drifted off to sleep.

Jake was up well before the sun came up. He strapped his gun on then went to the kitchen of the boarding house. Sharon had been baking breakfast rolls and was taking them out of the oven just as Jake walked into the kitchen.

"You're up early," she said with a smile. "Breakfast isn't ready yet."

"I have to get to work early this morning."

"What's going on?"

"I'm not sure," Jake replied, not wanting to explain what he thought was going to happen.

"Well, you better take a couple of these breakfast rolls with you. You can't go to work on an empty stomach."

Sharon wrapped up two warm breakfast rolls in a cloth napkin and handed them to him. Jake took the breakfast rolls.

"Thank you. I'll bring the napkin back to you later."

"See that you do," she said with a smile.

Jake smiled at her then turned and left the kitchen. As he walked out of the boarding house, he looked up at the sky. There were hints of light off to the east. He knew that the sun would be up soon. A look at his pocket watch showed him that it would be at least an hour before the livery stable would open for business. Joe would be up at sunup to take care of the animals that were in his care.

Jake walked down the street to the marshal's office. He entered the marshal's office and sat down at the desk to eat his breakfast rolls. He ate his breakfast while he thought about what might happen this morning.

Jake was not sure that the men who came into town yesterday were going to rob the bank. All he had was his gut feeling. His plan was to be ready for what might happen in an effort to prevent it. If nothing happened, then no harm done.

As soon as Jake finished his breakfast rolls, he took a double barrel shotgun off the gun rack in the office. He put a couple of shells in it and put a few more shells in his pocket. He then walked out of the marshal's office. Jake went down the street to the narrow space between the bank and another building, putting himself right next to the bank. He hunkered down behind a wood box that was used to hold cut wood for the stoves in the stores when the weather was cold.

While Jake waited, he looked up at the sky. It looked like it was going to be a nice day. Jake was not usually up this early. He usually worked late keeping the peace until the saloons closed. He soon discovered that it was very quiet this early in the morning.

As he leaned against the wood box, he noticed the early morning quiet was suddenly broken by the sound of boots on the boardwalk. Jake looked over the wood box to see who was up so early. Across the street, he saw the same men he had seen yesterday. They were walking toward the livery stable. They stopped and looked toward the front of the bank. A couple of them smiled before they began to move on.

As they began to walk along the boardwalk, one of the men turned, stepped off the boardwalk then walked across the street. The others waited to see what he was going to do. The one who crossed the street stepped up on the boardwalk in front of the bank, walked up to the front window, cupped his hands against the window and looked inside. Now Jake was sure they were going to rob the bank.

"Anybody inside?" the one who had gone into the bank yesterday asked.

"Don't see no one," the man at the window said, then turned and rejoined the others.

"It's still early. Let's get our horses," the one who seemed to be the leader said.

Jake could hear them walking along the boardwalk in the direction of the livery stable. He looked up at the second story windows of the Red Garter Saloon. He noticed that the curtain in one of the windows was drawn back, and the window was open. He waved his hand in the hope of finding out if John was there and ready. He was not surprised when he saw John wave back. All was ready for whatever might happen, at least as ready as they could be.

As time went by, Jake was growing impatient for something to happen. It seemed that he had been waiting for hours, but it was actually only about twenty to thirty minutes. He quickly sat up when he heard horses coming along the street from the direction of the livery stable. Being careful to stay out of sight, he looked around the edge of the wood box. He could see the five men slowly riding toward the bank. He noticed they were looking around in an apparent effort to see if anyone was around.

When they got to the bank, they turned in toward the bank. The one who had been in the bank yesterday got off his horse and handed the reins to one of the other men. A second man stepped out of the saddle and handed the reins of his horse to the same rider.

Jake watched. The fact that the two riders who dismounted and had not tied their horses to the hitching rail, convinced Jake they were there to rob the bank as soon as it opened. Jake laid his shotgun across the top of the wood box. He was ready.

The two men stood on the boardwalk in front of the bank looking around. They suddenly turned around and looked at the front of the bank when the front door opened. Looking around the wood box, Jake caught a glimpse of the bank owner as he held the door for the two men and invited them into the bank.

It was quiet. The two men had been in the bank for close to fifteen minutes when one came out with a canvas bag. He ran to his horse and swung into the saddle just as the second man backed out of the bank. The second man who came out of the bank fired two shots into the bank, then turned and ran to his horse.

Jake stood up, stepped up to the corner of the bank and fired both barrels of the shotgun at the men. Two horses bolted. The two riders, one now on the ground and one still on his horse turned and started shooting toward Jake. The man who was still on a horse was thrown from the horse and landed on the ground in front of the bank. As he started to get up, he was hit by a shot from John. The other one on foot turned around and ducked back into the bank.

Shots rang out from the second story window of the saloon. One more man was dropped. John fired a couple of shots at the one who was able to spur his horse toward the edge of town, but his missed.

The one who was getting away raced down the street toward the edge of town, he was greeted by Joe Wilcox, the blacksmith, at the livery stable. Joe had been watching the gunfight in front of the bank. When the shooting started, he grabbed his shotgun and stepped out in front of his stable. He saw the man riding toward him, took aim and fired as soon as the bank robber got close enough. The man and his horse took the full blast of the shotgun, blowing the robber out of his saddle, killing him instantly. It also put the horse down.

When Jake saw what happened to the man who was getting away, he turned his attention to the one man who was pinned down in the bank. He knew there was a backdoor to bank. With all the others dead or wounded, Jake turned and ran to the back of the bank. He arrived just in time to see the man had left the bank by the backdoor. The man ran down behind the next building then turned and ran back toward the street.

Jake remembered seeing a horse tied to the hitching rail in front of the Mercantile Store only a couple of buildings down from the bank. He quickly ran back between the buildings just in time to see the man untying the horse and was about to put his foot in the stirrup. Jake stopped, leaned up against the corner of the building and took careful aim. He fired two shots at the bank robber. The first one hitting his arm causing him to let go of the horse. Jake's second shot hit him in the back as he tried to run for cover.

The man slowly turned then fell to the ground. Jake walked up beside the man, keeping his gun ready in case the man had any fight left in him. Jake found he was still alive, but his breathing was shallow and labored. Jake knelt down beside the man.

"What's your name?" Jake asked.

The man just looked up at him for a second, coughed, then spit up some blood.

"My tombstone," he said, then coughed again, "should read - - - Jacob - - Runyon."

Jake nodded, then watched Jacob smile. The smile slowly faded from his face as he breathed his last.

Of the five men who had come to Hill City to rob the bank, four of them were dead and one was seriously injured. The injured man was taken to the doctor's office for treatment but he was not expected to live. The teller at the bank had been shot, but he was going to survive and be able to return to work within a few days, although he would be limited in the use of his left arm for at least a mouth.

The horses that had received injuries were treated by Joe at the livery stable. All the horses were expected to recover except one. Joe was given ownership of the five horses in payment for their care.

As soon as the streets were cleared of the bodies and injured horses, things quickly returned to normal. People began to return to doing their business.

Jake and John returned to the marshal's office where they sat down and had a cup of coffee. They talked about what had happened, then decided that since Jake was up the earliest he should go get some rest. He would come to work for the evening shift and John would go home early. All was quiet in the little town of Hill City once again.

CHAPTER TEN

The Theft of the Army Payroll

A small detachment of Army soldiers from Fort Meade rode up in front of the marshal's office in Hill City in late July. They looked like they had been riding hard, and for some time. The young lieutenant dismounted from his horse, stepped up on the boardwalk, straightened his uniform then entered the marshal's office.

John was sitting at his desk and had seen the detachment of soldiers ride up in front of his office. He had no idea why they were there, but figured he would find out soon enough.

"Welcome to Hill City," John said with a smile as the young lieutenant stepped into the marshal's office. "I'm Marshal Walker.

"This is not a social call, Marshal," the young lieutenant said rather sharply. "We are here on business."

"Okay, but do you mind telling what your name is before we get down to whatever business you have with me?"

"I'm Second Lieutenant William Collins of the Eighth Cavalry, of the United States Army stationed at Fort Meade, in the Dakota Territory," he said with the sharpness of someone who was extremely proud of his position.

"Now, what is your business with me?"

"We are looking for two soldiers who deserted their post and stole the Army payroll at Fort Meade. We believe the two soldiers have come to your town."

"What makes you think they are here?" John asked, just as Jake walked in the door.

"What's going on," Jake asked seeing the look on John's face and the lieutenant.

"The lieutenant is looking for two of his soldiers who stole the Army payroll and deserted. He thinks they came here."

"I haven't seen any soldiers," Jake said rather casually.

"And who are you, sir?" the lieutenant asked Jake in a demanding tone.

"He's Jake Murdock, and he's my deputy. Anything you have to say to him, you can say to me," John said harshly, not liking the way the lieutenant spoke to Jake.

The lieutenant looked at John before he spoke again.

"The two men we are looking for stole the Army payroll, killed the two guards on duty at the payroll office then stole two Army horses. The tracks we were able to find led toward here."

"I have not seen any Army horses, or anyone who might look like he was a soldier around town," Jake said.

"Well, it is unlikely they would be wearing their uniforms," the lieutenant said sarcastically.

"If they are deserters, I wouldn't expect they would, but they might be carrying side arms like the military uses, or their horses would have Army brands, or they might still have military saddles. Even their clothes might give away the fact they were uniforms due to their color which might show where the gold strip down the side of the pants had been removed," Jake said looking right at the young lieutenant who appeared to be only a couple of years older than himself.

"You said their tracks led in this direction. Did you follow them into town?" John asked.

"Well, no. We lost their tracks about a mile or so outside of town."

"Then you have no idea where they went. Is that correct?" John asked.

"Well, no. We, or I, just assumed they would come into town to get supplies."

"That was probably a fair assumption, but I'm afraid it was not the right one," John said, then turned to look at Jake.

"Jake, why don't you ride out to where the lieutenant last saw the tracks of the two deserters. Maybe you can help them figure out where the deserters went," John suggested.

"If the lieutenant doesn't mind, I'd be glad to help them, if I can."

The young lieutenant looked at Jake for a moment. He was thinking Jake looked a little young to have the experience of a good tracker.

John was the kind of lawman who didn't miss much. He noticed the way the lieutenant looked at Jake.

"I wouldn't judge my deputy by his age, Lieutenant," John said seeing the look on the lieutenant's face. "He's not only an excellent tracker, he is also very good with a gun."

The lieutenant looked at John, but didn't say anything.

"I might suggest you take your horses over to the stable and get them some feed and water. They look like they are about done in," Jake suggested. "It could be a long trek before we catch up with them."

The lieutenant looked at Jake, then looked out the window. It was clear that he was thinking about what Jake had said. The lieutenant turned back and looked at Jake again before walking to the door and calling his sergeant.

Jake could hear him giving his sergeant orders. He noticed the sergeant passed the orders to the rest of the soldiers, then saw them leading their horses toward the livery stable.

"Take your men down the street to the café and get something to eat. It could prove to be the last decent meal they get for awhile," John said. "As soon as you are done eating and your horses have been fed and watered, Jake will go with you. It looks like you need a good tracker."

"Thank you. The Army will reimburse you for his time."

"Jake, you might want to go have something to eat with them. It will give you a chance to get to know the men in his patrol.

"Yes, sir," Jake said, winked at John then walked out the door.

"Lieutenant, Jake is good at what he does. Show him the respect he deserves, and you will not only get along, but you will probably get your deserters and the payroll back. If you don't, he will probably leave you on your own while he finds the deserters and your payroll," John said.

"Yes, sir," the lieutenant said, then turned and walked out the door.

John shook his head. He hoped that the young lieutenant paid close attention to Jake. It was obvious that he could learn a lot from Jake about what it is like out here in the frontier. It was clear that the lieutenant didn't know much about tracking.

After the soldiers and Jake had eaten their lunch, they walked down to the livery stable. As the soldiers saddled their horses, the lieutenant looked at the buckskin horse that Jake was saddling. He walked over to Jake.

"Excuse me, but are you planning on riding that horse?" Lieutenant Collins asked.

Jake turned and looked at the lieutenant. He wondered why the lieutenant would ask such a question since he was obviously saddling the horse.

"Yes. Why do you ask?"

"He doesn't look like a horse that can withstand the rigors of a long hard ride."

"Sir, this horse can not only withstand the rigors of a long hard ride, he will still be going when the horses you have quit."

"Suit yourself," the lieutenant said as he turned and walked back to his horse.

Jake chuckled to himself as he swung into the saddle. He reached down and patted his horse on its neck while he waited for the soldiers to mount up.

With the lieutenant positioned in front of the troops, he looked to see if everyone was ready.

"Lead on, Lieutenant. You have to show me where you lost the tracks of the deserters."

The lieutenant looked at Jake with disgust, then raised his arm.

"Forward," the lieutenant called out then began riding down the street. He was followed by his troops.

Jake rode alongside the sergeant, directly behind the lieutenant. Nothing was said for awhile, but Jake noticed that the sergeant kept looking at him. Jake turned and looked at the sergeant.

"Do you have something you want to say to me, Sergeant?" Jake asked quietly.

"Well, sir, the lieutenant is new to the frontier. He's trying to prove himself. He has a lot to learn."

"I understand. I just hope he lives long enough to learn it."

"So do I," the sergeant replied.

With that said, nothing more was said until they came to the last place that the patrol had seen the tracks of the two deserters. The lieutenant raised his arm and called for the patrol to halt. Jake rode up alongside the lieutenant.

"These are the last tracks we saw of the deserters," Lieutenant Collins said as he pointed to the ground.

Jake looked at the ground for a moment, then stepped out of the saddle. He stepped in front of his horse and knelt down to study the tracks. The ground was fairly hard, but there was very little grass or weeds growing in the road. He looked up in the direction that the tracks were headed.

Jake stood up and began walking alongside the track. They were headed in the direction of Hill City. He walked along the tracks for several hundred feet with the lieutenant and his patrol following along behind Jake. Jake stopped suddenly and looked off to the west.

"Excuse me, but we will never catch them if we are going to chase them on foot," the lieutenant said sarcastically.

Jake turned and looked at the lieutenant and the sergeant before he spoke.

"We'll never catch them if we don't take the time to find where they left the road. Right here is where one of them left the road and headed west into those trees."

The lieutenant looked off to the west, then looked back at Jake.

"Where did the other one go?" the lieutenant asked.

"He continued down the road. My guess would be that he also left the road, but further on down. They will probably join up again somewhere west of here, would be my guess."

"Why did they split up only to join up again? It makes no sense."

"I'm afraid you will have to ask them."

"Do you have some idea of why they might have split up?"

"My best guess would be to make it harder for you to follow them. I think it was probably their plan to get you to believe they had gone into Hill City, when they actually turned west and went deeper into the hills, probably heading for Wyoming."

"Sergeant, you take three men and go after the first one who turned off. I'll take the rest of the men and go after the other one," the lieutenant said.

"You can do that if you want, but - - - -," Jake said but was interrupted before he could finish.

"You are absolutely correct. I can do what I want," the lieutenant said sharply.

"Fine, that's your choice. I'll be returning to Hill City. Good luck," Jake said as he walked up beside his horse, put his foot in the stirrup and swung into the saddle.

"You will be going with me. That's an order," Lieutenant Collins said sharply.

"I don't work for you and I'm not one of your soldiers. I'm not obligated to follow your commands."

"I paid you to track them."

"I found their tracks," Jake said then turned and looked at the sergeant. "Sergeant, did you see me get any pay for this?"

"No, sir," the sergeant said reluctantly.

"Sergeant, is there a reward for the capture of the two deserters?" Jake asked.

"Yes, sir."

"In that case, I'll go find them and bring them in. Lieutenant, you can do it your way."

"Lieutenant Collins, I think it would be in your best interest to do as Mr. Murdock says. How do you think it will look if he brings in the deserters while we're still out here looking for them, sir?"

The lieutenant started to say something to the sergeant, but quickly stopped himself before he said something stupid. He knew the sergeant would have to report what happened to the major at Fort Meade. He also knew the sergeant was right.

"Sir, we could learn a lot from Mr. Murdock," the sergeant added.

Lieutenant Collins looked at Jake. It was clear that he didn't like being told what to do by a civilian, or by an enlisted man, but he had to admit to himself that the sergeant was right. It would look bad for him.

"Mr. Murdock, I would appreciate it if you would continue to help us find and arrest the deserters," the lieutenant said, his tone much more agreeable.

"I will continue to help you look for the deserters, but only if you and your men follow my instructions."

The lieutenant didn't like the terms. He looked at his men and realized that he didn't really have a choice. In the short time he had been on the frontier, he had made a number of mistakes. So far, they had not cost the lives of any of his men, but a few of them had been rather embarrassing. Maybe it was time to learn from someone who knew the frontier a lot better than he did.

"I agree with your terms. I hope this misunderstanding will be overlooked."

"I think we can work together to reach our common goal of capturing the deserters and getting the Army payroll back," Jake said. "This is what we are going to do. We are going to follow the second set of tracks. We need to be very careful."

"Why the second set of tracks?" the lieutenant asked in a tone that indicated he really wanted to learn as much as he could from Jake.

"It's my guess, and it is just a guess, that the second set of tracks will join up with the first set somewhere west of here where they will set up camp for the night. They may already have supplies, a change of clothes and fresh horses waiting for them. The splitting up was done in the hope you would lose their trail. It worked, at least for a little while," Jake explained.

"We will move out. Travel in single file. Keep as quiet as possible and keep your eyes open. And lieutenant, it is okay for you to use hand signals, but don't yell out commands. We don't need to let them know we are on to them."

The lieutenant nodded to Jake, then raised his arm and signaled to his men to follow. Without a sound, the troops moved out and followed Jake.

As soon as Jake saw where the second set of tracks left the road, he pointed them out to the lieutenant. Jake turned off the road and followed the tracks with the soldiers following along behind him. It was only about a hundred yards or so after they rode in among the trees that Jake stopped and turned in his saddle to see the lieutenant. He motioned for the lieutenant to ride up alongside him.

"Pass the word that there is to be no talking." Jake said quietly.

The lieutenant nodded his head, then turned to his sergeant signaled him to be quiet. As soon as the word was passed on, Jake turned back around and started moving again into the forest. He followed a deer trail through the forest that the tracks seemed to follow. The patrol followed along behind. The going was slow as Jake didn't want to be surprised, he wanted to be the one doing the surprising.

Jake and the patrol worked their way through the forest for several miles without hearing or seeing anything. It was slowly getting darker as the sun set, making it harder to see the tracks left by the second rider.

It wasn't long before Jake noticed that the tracks of the first rider joined those of the second rider. Jake raised his hand in the air for the troops to stop. Lieutenant Collins rode up next to Jake.

"Did you see something?" Lieutenant Collins asked in a whisper.

"The tracks from the first rider joined up with the tracks we have been following right here. It looks like they are riding together now. Since it is getting dark, we could come up on them pretty soon. Pass the word for everyone to stay alert and stay quiet."

The lieutenant nodded then turned around and told his sergeant to pass the word on, but quietly. The sergeant did as he was instructed.

"It won't be long before it will be too dark to follow them, and too dark to see where we are going." Lieutenant Collins whispered.

"I'm counting on that. Have everyone dismount. We will be walking for awhile."

Lieutenant Collins wasn't sure about what Jake was doing, but he would keep his word and follow Jake's instructions.

As soon as all the troopers were on the ground, Jake started walking. They walked along for almost an hour. It was getting too dark to go any further when Jake got just a whiff of smoke. He stopped then turned and looked at Lieutenant Collins and smiled

"Bring your sergeant up here," Jake whispered.

The lieutenant motioned for the sergeant to join them. The sergeant walked up next to Jake.

"Sergeant, do you smell smoke?" Jake asked in a whisper.

He sniffed the air and smiled, then nodded his head.

"Get rid of all the gear you are carrying. Just take a handgun with you. Move toward where the smoke is coming from and see if it is the men we are looking for. Don't do anything, just find out if it is them, then get back here as fast as you can without making a sound. Do you understand?"

"Yes, sir."

The sergeant took off his gun belt and yellow neckerchief and handed them to Lieutenant Collins. The sergeant looked at his lieutenant, nodded that he was ready then turned and looked at Jake. Jake nodded then watched the sergeant turn and disappear into the darkness with his pistol in his hand.

As soon as the sergeant was out of sight, Jake sat down next to a tree and leaned back against it. The lieutenant did the same after motioning the rest of the patrol to spread out a little and sit down at the base of trees. Once they were seated, most of the patrol set with their rifles across their laps. Although they were resting, they were keeping watch for anything that might cause them trouble. It was a time to wait.

Time passed slowly. Everyone was getting nervous and wondering about the sergeant, but they had not heard anything to indicate that the sergeant had run into trouble. As the time passed, several of the soldiers were getting worried that the sergeant might have been captured or worse.

It was almost one in the morning when they heard the faint sound of something moving toward them. The sergeant was being as quiet as he could as he walked right past Jake.

"Sergeant," Jake whispered.

The sergeant turned and looked at Jake before he spoke, "I'm glad to see you."

"What did you find out," Jake asked quietly.

"Well, sir, there are four men not two."

"Four?" the lieutenant asked.

"Yes, sir. There was Wilson and Beatty from the fort, and two other men I've never seen before. You were right, Mr. Murdock. Wilson and Beatty had changed clothes. Their uniforms were laying on the ground next to the campfire. It looked like they are planning on burning 'um. I noticed what looked like two western saddles sitting on the ground only a few feet from their campfire. It was hard to see for sure."

"Did you see any others," Jake asked.

"No sir. They seemed pretty relaxed as if they didn't know we were here."

"It looks like they had this all planned out. A change of clothes and saddles so no one would think they were soldiers," Jake said. "Could you tell if they were changing horses?"

"No sir, but the horses looked like the ones they used to get away on."

"What do we do now?" Lieutenant Collins asked Jake.

"How easy is it to get around behind them?" Jake asked the sergeant."

"Well, sir, I don't know. It looked like they might have had their backs to a rock wall, but I could only see a little of it. It was about ten or fifteen feet behind them so the light from the fire didn't light it up very well."

Jake thought for a minute as he looked at the ground in front of him. He looked up at the lieutenant for a moment before he said anything.

"Lieutenant, I think we should let the men rest for awhile."

"We're not going to attack them now?" the lieutenant said with a hint of surprise in his voice.

"We are going to give them a chance to relax and get comfortable. In the meantime, we are going to give your men a chance to get a little rest before we attack them, and hopefully surprise them," Jake said with a smile.

"Will we attack them just before dawn?"

"Yes. Just as soon the sky starts to get light in the east."

"Sergeant, I might suggest you post two guards, one to the left of that tree over there," Jake said pointing to a rather large tree. "One to the right of that tree over near the horses, then get some rest."

"Yes sir."

"Lieutenant, sack out for a couple of hours. I'll keep watch."

Lieutenant Collins simply nodded then sat down and leaned back against a tree.

Jake stood up and moved out in front of the soldiers about twenty feet. Leaning against a tree, he just stood there and listened and watched. He heard an owl in a tree about fifty feet away. The only other sounds were from the shuffling of the horses' hooves in the soft pine needles that covered the ground when they moved while sleeping.

Time passed slowly. It seemed like forever before there was a changing of the guards. Jake looked back at the soldiers when the guards were changed. Other than that, there was nothing but quiet.

When the time came to wake the soldiers, Jake went to the soldier standing guard nearest to him.

"Wake everyone, but do it quietly," Jake said. "Wake Lieutenant Collins first."

"Yes sir."

Jake watched as the soldier went to Lieutenant Collins and woke him. The lieutenant got up and walked over to Jake.

"It's time to get into position," Jake whispered. "We are going to walk up to their camp. If they have a guard posted, we will want to take him out first, and quietly. We will circle their camp before we wake them. Got it?"

"Yes."

"Good. I'll take the sergeant with me and half the men. I'll circle around to the left side. You take the right side. Be damn careful where you're shooting. I would not like it one bit if I get shot by you or one of your men."

"I'll do my best not to shoot any of our people."

"Good, but try not to let any of them escape. If one does, don't chase him. It will still be dark in the forest. That's a sure way to get yourself shot. We'll track him down when it gets light."

"I understand," the lieutenant said.

"Good luck, Collins."

"Good luck to you," Lieutenant Collins said as he stuck his hand out.

Jake looked at his hand, then reached out and shook it. They then got the men together and started moving to their positions.

The sky was just starting to get light in the east when they were ready. They had encircled the camp and had not found any guards posted which made it easier for them. They waited. Corporal Wilson was the first one to wake up. The corporal rolled over and sat up on his bedroll. As he stretched to get the stiffness out of his muscles, he suddenly froze. Only a few feet from him was a soldier with his rifle pointed at him. The soldier motioned for him not to make a sound.

On the other side of where the campfire had been, Private Beatty woke and sat up. He looked over at Wilson. Beatty thought there was something wrong because Wilson didn't move.

"Wilson, what's wrong?"

Without moving, Wilson said, "We've got company."

"Don't anyone move unless you plan to die right here and right now," Jake announced. "We have you surrounded and there's no way out."

The other two men sat up and looked around. All they could see were soldiers with guns pointed at them.

"Everyone standup with hands on the top of your heads. Anyone who does not comply with my instructions will be shot," Lieutenant Collins said.

Slowly, each of the four men stood up and put their hands on top of their heads. Several of the soldiers moved in and began putting the prisoners in shackles. Once they were secure and had been searched for weapons, they were lined up and sat down with guards standing behind them.

Jake and Collins searched the belongings of the four. They found the Army payroll.

As soon as all was secure, the campfire was relit and breakfast was prepared for all. The prisoners were fed by the soldiers. When breakfast was done, the fire was put out and the prisoners were tied in the saddles of their horses.

They were taken to Hill City where the two men who were not soldiers were put in jail. Once they were in jail, Lieutenant Collins took a minute to thank Jake for his help in capturing the deserters and recovering the Army payroll.

After they shook hands, the Army patrol took the two soldiers back to Fort Meade where they would be court-martialed. After the court-martial, they would be sent to an Army prison to be hung for murdering the guards at Fort Meade.

Upon the return to Hill City, it was discovered that the two civilians were wanted for robbery and murder in the Nebraska Territory. Jake took them to Lincoln, Nebraska where they were tried in a civilian court. They were found guilty and hung for their crimes.

Jake received the reward for the capture of the two who had killed a bank teller and robbed the bank. After receiving the reward from the bank in Nebraska, Jake returned to Hill City where he returned to work as a deputy marshal.

Shortly after Jake returned from Nebraska, he received an envelope from Lieutenant Collins. In the envelope was a letter thanking him for his help in capturing the two deserters and a bank draft paying him for his help in capturing them?

Jake deposited the bank draft and the reward in the local bank. He now had enough money to buy some cattle and a ranch, but no one to share it with. He decided to stay on as a deputy in Hill City and work with his friend, John, for a while longer.

CHAPTER ELEVEN

The Killing of a Pinkerton Detective

It was a quiet day in late August. The weather had been unusually hot for the past couple of days in the Black Hills. The stagecoach from Sturgis, on its way to Custer City, had just rolled into Hill City. The horses were covered with lather and looked to be exhausted. It was obvious that they had been driven hard and for some distance.

Jake was sitting in his chair in front of the marshal's office where he had been trying to keep cool, but with little success. He turned and looked down the street when he heard the stagecoach driver yelling for the horses to stop. Jake immediately noticed the condition of the horses. He stood up and began walking down the street toward the stage station.

The driver of the stagecoach had pulled the team of horses to a stop and was scrambling down from his seat. As soon as he was on the ground, he quickly tied the lead horses to the hitching rail. He turned to head for the marshal's office when he saw Jake coming toward him.

"We need Doc," the driver called out, a little short of breath.

Jake looked over at the saloon and saw Alice, one of the working girls, standing in the doorway of the Silver Dollar Saloon watching what was going on.

"Alice, run get the doctor," Jake called out.

Alice acknowledged she had heard him with a nod, then immediately turned and ran toward the doctor's office. Jake ran up to the stagecoach and opened the door.

Sitting on the floor of the stagecoach was a woman in a very nice dress holding a man. The man's head was in her lap, but the woman was looking at Jake. There were tears running down the woman's face, and there was blood all over the front of the woman's dress.

"Are you hurt, ma'am," Jake asked.

"No," she cried. "Mr. Booker is dead. I tried to help him. I really tried to help him."

"I'm sure you did, ma'am," Jake said then turned around to get some help.

Several people had gathered around to see what had happened. Jake saw several local men standing on the boardwalk. He enlisted a couple of them to help remove Mr. Booker from the stagecoach. As soon as Mr. Booker was out of the stagecoach, they took him over to Doc's office.

Jake reached out a hand to help the woman out of the stagecoach. As she stepped out, she slipped on the step of the stagecoach, falling toward him. She wrapped her arms around his neck to keep from falling as Jake caught her. He wrapped his arms around her to keep her from falling to the ground.

When she got her footing, she looked into his eyes for a moment before she took her arms from around Jake's neck. He immediately let her go.

"I'm sorry," she said.

"It's okay," Jake said as he turned and walked her to a bench in front of the stage station.

John showed up just as the woman let go of Jake. He smiled at Jake.

"That's the hard way to meet a girl," John said as Jake turned to look at him.

"I didn't meet her. She simply slipped."

"If you say so," John said as he turned and looked at the woman.

"What do we have here?" John asked, turning serious when he saw the blood on the woman's dress.

"I'm not sure what happened, but we have one dead man and a woman covered with his blood. I had the body taken over to Doc's office."

"I'll talk to the lady to see what she can tell us. You talk to the driver and find out what happened."

"Okay," Jake said.

Jake took a minute to look around. He saw the driver sitting on another bench at the far end of the stage station. He was leaning forward with his elbows on his knees and his face in his hands. He leaned back and looked up when Jake walked up to him. The driver looked exhausted. Jake sat down beside him.

"You want to tell me what happened out there?"

"Yeah. We was comin' around a bend in the road about two, maybe three miles back down the road when someone started shootin' at us. Mr. Booker was hit in the head, but he didn't die right away. Mrs. Armor held him on the floor of the stagecoach while I skedaddled out ta there. We took a couple of shots in the back of the stagecoach, but they didn't hit no one," the driver explained.

"Was there any attempt to get you to stop?"

"No, sir. There weren't none. I didn't hear anyone call out for us to stop, and I didn't see no one tryin' to chase us. He just shot at us," the driver said, still trying to understand what really happened.

"Were you carrying anything of value?" Jake asked.

"No, sir. At least, not that I know about. I'm usually told when there's anythin' of value on the stagecoach. When there's somethin' of value, I usually have someone ridin' shotgun."

"They made no attempt to stop you?" Jake asked wondering why there had been no attempt to stop the stagecoach.

"No, sir. None at all. Now that I've had a chance to think on it some, there was only one shootin' at us."

"Only one?" Jake asked.

"Yeah. Only one shooter shootin' at us."

Jake looked at the driver for a few seconds. What he was being told by the driver didn't seem to make any sense, that was until Jake came up with a possible reason.

"Do you have any idea what Mr. Booker did for a living, or who he worked for?"

"Well, I don't know for a fact, but I heard tell he was an important man."

"Where did you hear that?"

"I heard it in Silver City. He was talkin' to the sheriff there. We had a short layover for fresh horses and lunch."

"Did you hear who he worked for?"

"I overheard some guy tell this other fella that he was some kind of a lawman, but didn't say who he worked for or where he was from. I picked him up in Sturgis."

"Jake, could you come hear for a moment?" John called out, interrupting Jake's questioning of the stagecoach driver.

"Yeah. Don't go anywhere," Jake said to the driver. "I'll be right back."

"I'll be right here."

Jake turned and walked over to John. John looked around before speaking to Jake.

"I talked to Mrs. Armor. She couldn't tell us much that would help find the shooter. She doesn't know the country around here," John said, then looked around before saying anything else.

"Jake, Mr. Booker was a Pinkerton Detective."

"You're kidding?"

"No. He was coming here to see me."

"To see you?"

"Yeah. It seems there is a train robber and killer living right under our noses. The robber killed two guards on a train that was going east from Sturgis with a shipment of gold. It seems the killer lives here, or at least near here.

Booker was coming to talk to me to tell me who it was, and for me to help him capture the man."

"Who is it?"

"I don't know. He didn't want to send me a letter or a telegram with the man's name on it for fear someone would see it and alert the man."

"Did he have the man's name on him?"

"I went over to Doc's and took the papers from Booker's coat. Nothing in the papers in his coat pockets gave me even a hint as to who he was here to capture. There is no mention of the man by name, or anything about him," John said then looked around. "Keep it under your hat for now."

"Sure. Not having a name is going to make it hard to figure out who we are to arrest. By the way, the driver thinks there was only one shooter."

"No kidding," John said with a hint of frustration in his voice. "About the only thing we can do is to go to where the stagecoach was shot at, and see if we can find anything that will help us figure out who the shooter is and where he went.

"I want you to go out there. You're a good tracker. I suggest you get started as soon as you can, and be careful," John said.

Jake nodded that he understood, then turned and walked back over to the driver of the stagecoach.

"Can you give me some idea where you were shot at?"

"You going back there?"

"Yes."

"Well, let's see," the driver said then took a minute to think about it. "I had just come around a curve in the road. It was where there's a narrow place in the road. Coming up this way, there's a place where there's a cliff about forty or so feet high on the left side of the road. It would be on the right side going from here. On the other side of the road was a shorter rise, only about ten, maybe twelve feet high.

I guess it is sort of like a pass through there, but a short one.

"The road is crooked around there and we have to slow down some. We was shot at just as we passed between them little cliffs. The shots come from the lower side, the same side Mr. Booker was sittin' on in the stagecoach. As I recall from what Mrs. Armor said, Mr. Booker was sittin' on that side of the stagecoach and he was lookin' out when he was shot."

"Mrs. Armor was the woman holding him when you arrived here?"

"Yeah."

"Thanks," Jake said. "I have a pretty good idea where the shooting took place."

Jake walked back over to John. John was talking to Mrs. Armor.

"Excuse me," Jake said. "I'm going out to where the stagecoach was shot at before it gets too dark."

"Okay, but be careful," John said.

Jake nodded then walked toward the boarding house. He went to his room in the boarding house and got a few things he thought he might need, then went to the livery stable. As soon as he had his horse saddled, his supplies in his saddlebags, his rifle in the saddle scabbard, and a bedroll tied to his saddle, he mounted up and rode out of town.

It took a little over an hour for Jake to find the place where the stagecoach had been attacked. He found tracks in the dirt road where the horses had suddenly increased their pace. That gave Jake an idea of where the shooter had been when he fired at the stagecoach.

Jake rode his horse off the road to a grassy area and tied him to a tree. As he stood by his horse looking around, he drew his gun then slipped it back in the holster very lightly. He moved away from his horse and began searching the ground around the base of the rocks. When he found nothing, he moved into the rocks. He was about ten feet above the road in the rocks when he found a cartridge case from a .30 caliber Winchester. It was shiny, indicating that it had not been there very long.

After a little more looking around, he found two more cartridge cases. He picked them up and put them in his pocket. It was clear that he had found the place where the shooter had been when he fired on the stagecoach.

It didn't take Jake long to figure out how the shooter had gotten to the place he had shot from. Jake followed the almost invisible path the shooter would have used. He followed it down out of the rocks. It only took him a couple of minutes to find where the shooter had tied his horse. The fact that the grass around the base of the tree had been eaten away, and that the horse had moved around the base of the tree indicated the shooter had been waiting for some time for the stagecoach to come by.

Jake knelt down and studied the tracks left by the horse's hooves very carefully. He wanted to be able to recognize the tracks if he should find the horse. Finding the horse would probably lead him to the shooter.

Jake returned to his horse, untied it, and then led his horse to where he had found the shooter's horse's tracks. He walked along until he came to a narrow trail. The tracks left by the horse turned onto the trail. Jake swung into the saddle and rode along the trail while keeping an eye on the tracks left on the trail.

The sun was getting ready to duck down behind a distant ridge. Jake knew it would soon be too dark to continue to follow the tracks. He also knew he was not very far from Silver City. It had become clear that the shooter was headed for Silver City, since it was the only town in the area. The only real question was, was he staying in Silver City, or did he continue on to someplace else. Jake would have to wait for the answer.

Jake was able to follow the tracks left by the shooter's horse into Silver City, but lost them in among the tracks on the main street of the small mining town. With nothing else he could do tonight, Jake rode up to the livery stable and stepped out of the saddle. The blacksmith stepped out of the barn and looked at Jake.

"There something I can do for you, young man?"

"I hope so. Did you have a rider come into town today? It would have been probably late afternoon. He was riding a horse that had a nail missing on the horse's right front hoof."

"That's a strange request. I take it you have been following him."

"That would be correct. I'm Jake Murdock, Deputy Marshal from Hill City."

"I've heard of you. I had a man come into town. He needed his horse shod. It had a loose shoe on the right front hoof."

"Is he still in town?"

"I would think so. I have his horse in my barn."

"May I look at the horse," Jake asked.

"Sure," the blacksmith said as he turned around.

Jake followed the blacksmith into the barn. When they stopped at a stall, the blacksmith pointed at the horse. Jake walked up alongside the horse and lifted his front right leg. The horse still had the shoe with the missing nail. He turned and looked at the blacksmith.

"I told him that I could not shoe his horse today, but I would do it first thing in the morning," he said with a grin. "I need to make a new shoe for the horse."

"Can you tell me where the rider of this horse is now?"

"No. I suggested the boarding house down the street for a place for him to spend the night, but I don't know if he went there. He might be in one of the two saloons. He asked about where he might get a drink."

"Thanks. One more thing, can you tell me what he looks like?"

"Sure. He's about your height and build, has dark brown hair and handlebar mustache, and wears a black vest over a white shirt, and black pants. You should probably like to know that he carries his gun tied down, and has a small gun under the vest that is easy to reach but is hard to see," he said with a grin.

"Thanks, that's good to know," Jake said. "I'll put my horse up here if you don't mind. I'll take care of him. He doesn't like strangers touching him unless I'm with him so I'll rub him down. How much for a night and feed?"

"Four bits will do it."

Jake paid the blacksmith, put his horse in a stall then took care of his horse. When he was done, he walked out to the street and looked up and down it. He decided that he would go to the saloon on the same side of the street he was already on. If he wasn't there, he would go across the street and see if he was in the only other saloon in town.

As Jake approached the first saloon, he moved up close to the building. He slipped his hand over his gun, then slowly moved next to the window. Leaning against the building, he peered in the window. There were several men in the saloon, four of them playing cards in the far corner, one standing at the bar, and two others seated at a table with a bottle of whiskey on the table. They appeared to be just talking. None of the men in the bar fit the description the blacksmith had given Jake.

As Jake leaned back against the side of the building, he caught a glimpse of a flash of light off something from across the street. He quickly pulled back into the shadows just as a shot was fired at him. Jake scrambled around the corner of the saloon between the buildings as another bullet took out a small chunk of the corner of the building.

Jake ran to the back of the saloon then ran behind it to the other side. Standing at the back corner of the saloon, he looked across the street toward the space between the buildings where the shot had come from. He could just barely make out the shadow of someone between the buildings. It wasn't until the man turned and ran by a lighted window toward the back of the building that he was able to see him clearly.

Jake fired a shot at the man. He heard the man let out a cry of pain. Jake was not sure how badly the man was injured. He had to be careful. Jake waited for a moment and just listened, but couldn't hear anything.

Suddenly, he heard the sound of a horse running away. Since the man he had been chasing had his horse in the livery stable, he wasn't sure who had shot at him. If it was the man he was chasing, he must have stolen a horse that was behind the building. It didn't really matter who had taken a shot at him. He would find him.

With his gun in his hand, Jake moved along the side of the building. When he reached the front of the building, he looked around then sprinted across the street to the front of another building. He peeked around the corner into the space, but found it empty.

Jake leaned against the building as he slipped his gun into his holster. He heard someone running along the boardwalk toward him. From the lights from the windows in the buildings, he could see it was the town sheriff.

"I'm Randall Smith, the town sheriff. What's going on here?" he asked as he stopped in front of Jake.

"I'm Jake Murdock, Deputy Marshal from Hill City. Somebody took a shot at me. I'm not sure, but I think it was the man I followed here."

"I take it, he's wanted for something?"

"Yes. He's wanted for killing a Pinkerton Detective on the Sturgis to Custer City stagecoach. He would have passed through here yesterday."

"Do you have a name for this man?"

"No. I have no idea who he is or why he shot and killed the detective."

"That makes it kind of hard to find him."

"It does, but I have a description of him from your town's blacksmith."

"I heard a horse leaving town in a hurry," the sheriff said. "Was it the man you're looking for?"

"I think so, but it will have to wait until tomorrow before I can track him. I might add that I think he is wounded. I won't know until tomorrow when I check out the area where he was when I shot him," Jake said. "It's too dark to see anything now."

"Okay. Do you want help finding him?"

"No. I think it would be best if I track him alone. I'll start at first light."

"Okay. Have it your way," Sheriff Smith said then turned around and walked away.

Jake went down the street to the livery stable. The blacksmith was standing in the door to the barn when Jake arrived.

"I heard shots. Did you get your man?"

"No, but I think he is wounded," Jake said. "I'd like to spend the night in your barn. He escaped on a stolen horse. He might try to come back and get his horse."

"That would be a darn fool thing for him to do. His horse still has a loose shoe, and he knows it. If his horse was to throw a shoe, the guy would be walking and he'd have a lame horse."

"Any idea who's horse he might have taken?"

"Do you know where he got the horse?"

"Behind one of the saloons, I think it was the Eagle's Nest Saloon."

"If it's the horse that the barkeeper usually tied up there while he's working, the man who stole him ain't going very far. That old horse couldn't run more than a half mile before giving out. The barkeeper just rides him back and forth from his house to the bar. For some reason, he likes that old horse," the blacksmith said with a grin. "It's more like a pet to him."

"Well, I hope the horse isn't pushed too hard. I'd hate to see him kill the horse."

"You go right ahead and sleep in the loft of the barn, if you want. I doubt the man you're looking for will come back here. I'm calling it a night. Close the door when you go in. I'll be back at sunup."

As soon as the blacksmith left, Jake went into the barn and closed the barn door behind him. He took his bedroll off his saddle, then climbed up into the loft. After laying out his bedroll, he laid down and listened to the sounds of the night inside the barn then dozed off to sleep.

When a cock crowed somewhere out back of the barn, Jake sat up. He got up, rolled up his bedroll then climbed down from the loft. He saddled his horse, opened the barn door and led his horse outside. Jake had just tied his horse to the hitching rail when the blacksmith showed up. He was carrying a plate with a cloth over it and a cup of coffee.

"The wife thought you should have something to eat before you go."

"Thank you," Jake said as he took the plate and cup.

Jake sat down on a bale of hay to eat his breakfast of a thick slice of ham and three fried eggs and two biscuits. When he finished eating, he handed the cup and plate to the blacksmith and thanked him.

Jake untied his horse and began walking down behind the building to the place where he had shot the man who had shot at him. Near the back of one of the buildings, he found blood splatter on the wall of one of the buildings and some signs of blood on the ground. He also found a gun lying behind a wood box. He picked up the gun and put it in his saddlebags.

It was not hard to follow the footprints left in the dirt. They led to the tracks of a horse. It was clear that the man had gotten onto the horse and took off. The horse had left a very clear trail. Jake swung into the saddle and began following the tracks.

It wasn't very long and the tracks showed that the horse had turned off into the wood. Jake turned in and followed the tracks. As he followed the tracks, he saw several branches of trees that had blood on them. The man Jake shot had to be losing a lot of blood.

Jake suddenly reined up and looked down at the ground. From the tracks of the horse and look of the dirt next to where the horse had stopped, it was clear that the man had fallen off the horse and the horse had simply stopped then walked away.

Jake got off his horse and studied the tracks. In the dirt were signs that the rider had dragged himself off away from the narrow trail. All Jake could think about was it was like hunting a wounded animal. He had no idea what condition the injured man was in, or if there was any fight left in him. He would have to move carefully.

Jake drew his gun from his holster, then started slowly following the tracks on foot. He kept an eye out for the man in the hope of seeing him before he was seen.

Jake hadn't gone very far when he noticed a foot sticking out from behind a large boulder. He moved slowly toward the foot, keeping his gun ready. When he was only a couple of feet from the foot, he stopped and listened. He heard nothing. He moved a little closer and looked at the foot. It hadn't moved. From the angle of the foot there was no way the man could be waiting for him to come around that end of the boulder. The man would be in no position to shoot at him without turning over first. Jake readied himself. With his gun firmly in his hand, he stepped out from behind the boulder and pointed his gun at the man.

The man's gun was in his hand, and his hand was lying at his side. The man never moved. Jake moved up to him and took the gun from the man's hand. He then knelt down and turned the man over. He was dead. He had apparently bled to death in his attempt to escape.

With nothing else to do, Jake wrapped the man in his bedroll, then went looking for the horse. He found the horse only a little ways away. He put the man over the back of the horse then led it back to Silver City.

Jake rode down the street of Silver City to the sheriff's office. As he stepped out of the saddle, Sheriff Smith stepped out of his office.

"Well, I see you got your man."

"Yeah. He was dead when I found him. He had bled to death from his gunshot wound."

Sheriff Smith stepped off the boardwalk and lifted the man's head so he could see his face.

"This is Frank Grover. He's wanted for robbery, horse stealing and murder. There's a thousand-dollar reward for him dead or alive. Looks like you've got some money coming," the sheriff said as he looked up at Jake.

"I still don't know if this is the man I was following," Jake said. "The man I was after was reported as living in Hill City."

"I'm sure this is our man. The wanted poster on him was put out by the Pinkerton Detective Agency. It arrived just yesterday on the stagecoach. I didn't get a chance to look at it until this morning. I'll notify them that Frank Grover was brought in by you dead and positively identified. They'll send you the money within a couple of weeks."

After signing a paper for the sheriff, Jake said goodbye and headed back to Hill City. When he returned he told John all about what had taken place.

John found it interesting, but wasn't sure Jake had gotten the man who shot Mr. Booker. John sent off a wire to the Pinkerton Detective Agency letting them know about Frank Grover and asking if this was the man Mr. Booker had come to Hill City to arrest.

It only took a few hours before John received a reply. The Pinkerton Detective Agency confirmed that Frank Grover was the man Mr. Booker was coming to get. Mr. Booker believed that Grover lived in Hill City was why he had contacted Marshal Walker.

Jake received his reward about three weeks later with a letter from the Pinkerton Detective Agency expressing their appreciation for a job well done.

Jake returned to his job as the deputy marshal for Hill City. It didn't take long for things to return to normal.

CHAPTER TWELVE

Hunting the Bounty Hunter

The fall of the year had brought color to the hills around Hill City. The weather was cool at night and warm during the day. The town had seen very few fights and no shoot-outs over the past couple of months. It was almost as if peace had finally come to Hill City. That was until a young man rode into town on a pleasant September day.

The young man was clean shaven, but that was probably because he was young enough he didn't need to shave very often. He was dressed all in black from his flat brimmed hat with its silver hatband to his black cowboy boots with silver tips on the toes and fancy white stitching on the sides. He wore double holsters that were tied down on his legs. Even the holsters were black with fancy white stitching. In the holsters were a matching set of guns, each one was a fancy nickel-plated Colt .45 Peacemaker with mother of pearl grips. They were not the kind of guns that were seen very often in that part of the country because they were too expensive for the average cowboy or working man, and too nice to be carried around while working on a ranch or farm.

The horse the young man rode was black with four white stocking feet and a white blaze on its face. The saddle, bridle and saddlebags were also black. There was silver trim on the saddle, bridle and saddlebags. It was obvious that they were custom made, probably in Texas or Mexico, and would have cost a small fortune.

The young man sat straight in the saddle as if he was some sort of nobleman who owned the world, or at least a good part of it. He drew the attention of everyone who saw him as his horse walked along the street. He was like no one that most of the people of Hill City had ever seen.

John Walker was sitting at his desk in the marshal's office when he noticed the young man as he rode by. He caught only a glimpse of the young man, but his first impression was the young man was just a kid. It might have been because he didn't look a day older than sixteen.

John stood up and walked to the window. He had never seen such a sight. He wondered who this kid was, and what he was doing there. He looked out of place. He looked more like he belonged in one of those Wild West shows that impressed the people back east, but had little to do with what it was really like in the west.

He watched as the kid turned toward the hitching rail at the Golden Nugget Saloon. John walked out of the office and watched as the kid stepped out of the saddle, tied his horse to the hitching rail, then looked around. After a couple of minutes of just looking up and down the main street of town, the kid turned and walked into the saloon.

John left his office and hurried across the street to the Golden Nugget Saloon. When he got to the saloon, he stopped and looked in through the window. He could see one of the local trouble-makers was laughing at the kid. The kid didn't seem to like being the brunt of his jokes.

"What the hell are you supposed to be, kid?" Ben Miller asked while laughing at the way the young man was dressed.

"You keep talking like that and I'll show you who's a kid," he said looking Ben straight in the eyes.

Ben didn't know what to say. No one had ever talked back to him before.

"You little pip-squeak. I ought ta teach ya a lesson by paddlin' your butt and sendin' ya back to daddy."

"You try and you'll live just long enough to regret it," he said with a look that almost dared Ben to try something.

Just as it looked like Ben was going to draw on the kid, John drew his gun and stepped into the saloon.

"Ben, you draw that gun and I'll shoot you right where you stand."

Ben looked over at John and saw he had a gun in his hand, and it was pointed at him. After taking a breath, Ben relaxed and looked at the kid.

"I was only funnin' him," Ben said to John.

"You were egging him on. Now get out of here," John ordered.

"This ain't the end of this, kid" Ben said while looking at the kid.

"Ben, it better be, or you'll answer to me. Now get out of here before I toss you in jail to cool off."

Ben looked at John with disgust, then turned and left the saloon.

John waited until Ben had left the saloon before he put his gun in the holster. He walked up to the kid.

"You were about to pick a fight with one of the meanest men in town."

"He didn't scare me any, not in the least little bit," the kid said with an air of confidence.

"He should have. What's your name?"

"I'm Bill Adams," he said loud enough so everyone in the saloon could hear him.

"Well, Bill Adams, I don't know where you're from and I don't care, but out here you best be careful who you make mad. You make the wrong man mad and he'll kill you."

"I am not afraid of anyone. I came here looking for someone. I was told he lives here."

"Oh. Who you looking for?"

"I'm looking for a man by the name of Jake Murdock."

"What do you want with him?"

"I don't think that is any of your business, officer," the kid said sharply.

"What happens in this town, is my business," John said sharply.

"I just want to meet him. I've heard a lot about him."

"All you have to do is hang around the saloons. Eventually he'll find you. Right now, I think he's out of town."

"Oh. I was told I could find him here."

"Usually you can. It's a nice day. I think he went fishing. I take it he was not expecting you."

"No. He wasn't expecting me. Do you know where he is?"

"No, but he'll be back soon, probably just before dark."

"Thank you. I'll wait here for him. If you see him, please tell him I am here and would like to see him."

"I'll do that," John said.

John looked at Adams for a moment then turned and left the saloon. He returned to his office. Once he was in his office, he stood at the window and looked toward the Golden Nugget Saloon. From the way Adams acted in the saloon when he first walked in, John got the impression that Adams might just be a kid who thinks he's a gunfighter. But from the looks of him, it didn't look like he was anything more than just show. Everything about him showed John that the kid had probably read too many dime novels.

John had no idea where the kid learned about Jake. He wondered if the kid was going to try to make a reputation by killing Jake in a gunfight. John had a good chance to look at the kid. Everything the kid had looked new, like it had never been used before. Even his guns looked like they were new.

The thought of the dime novels caused John to remember he had read a couple of dime novels over the years. He seemed to remember reading one about a kid that tried to be a gunfighter, but lost his life when he took on the wrong man. If he remembered correctly, the picture on the front of the novel was of a young man dressed very much like Adams, and he was drawing against a cowboy.

The more he thought about the novel and Adams, the more ridiculous it all seemed. He certainly wasn't going to try to draw against someone like Jake, or was he? If nothing else, John needed to find Jake and let him know what was going on.

John went to the stable and got a horse. He watched his back trail to make sure that no one was following him. John rode out of town to a stream where he knew Jake liked to fish. He saw Jake sitting on a rock cooking something in a frying pan.

Jake heard John as he rode up. He watched as John got off his horse.

"What brings you out here? You looking for a little fresh fish for dinner?" Jake asked with a smile.

"Not really," John said as he tied his horse to a nearby tree.

"Well, since you're here, you might as well sit down and have supper with me. There's plenty for both of us, and the coffee's hot."

"I came to tell you there's a young man, really just a kid, looking for you."

"Oh. What's his name?"

"Bill Adams. Do you know him?"

"No, I don't think so.

"He talks like he's from back east somewhere."

"What's he want with me?" Jake said as he put a piece of fish on a plate for John.

"I'm not sure," John said as he took the plate. "I think he's here to make a name for himself by killing you."

Jake stopped suddenly and looked at John. He wasn't sure he had heard John correctly.

"Are you sure?"

"No, but he's dressed like he thinks he's a gunfighter. He carries two nickel-plated Colt .45s tied down on his legs. He hardly looks a day over sixteen. Can you think of anyone you might have killed or jailed that had a son, or a younger brother, who would be about sixteen by now?" John asked then took another bite of the fish."

"I suppose it's possible, but no one I know of."

"He said he was told that he could find you in Hill City."

"Any number of people know that I call Hill City home," Jake said.

"I'm sure you're right. Say, can I have another piece of fish," John asked as he held out his plate.

"Sure."

Jake put another piece of fish on the plate while he thought about what John had said. He knew that John was not one to get excited without reason. Jake wasn't looking for a gunfight with anyone, and he had no idea why this kid wanted to have a gunfight with him.

"John, do you really think he wants a gunfight with me?"

"He didn't come right out and say so, but that was the impression I got. It's fairly common knowledge that you are fast with a gun."

"People don't just go around looking for a gunfight. He's got to have a reason to want to have one with me. Wouldn't you think?" Jake asked.

"You'd think so, but maybe he has what he thinks is a reason. Maybe by killing you, he will get a reputation as someone who is fast with a gun. There's no way of knowing what someone like him thinks."

"I guess you could be right. What do you think I should do? I don't want a gunfight with some kid just because he wants to prove he's better, or faster than I am."

"Taking on the job of bounty hunter tends to give a person a reputation, especially if he's good at it. You have to admit, you are good at it. There's a lot of people out there who know you are fast with a gun," John said.

"What do you think I should do?" Jake asked.

"I think that is up to you, but I don't see many options."

"What do you mean?"

"You will have to face him sooner or later. If you leave, he will just follow you until he finds you."

"You think he is that set on having a gunfight with me?"

"He sure seems determined to do just that."

Jake sat there looking at the fish in his plate. He was trying to figure out what he should do.

"John, you think I could talk to this kid? Maybe, I could convince him that a shoot-out between us would prove nothing. If I kill him, it will just add to my reputation. If he kills me, he will end up with a reputation that will bring out everyone that wants to kill him for the same reason he wants to kill me. Eventually, someone will be faster and kill him. He'll be lucky to live to twenty-five."

"I doubt it will change his mind, but it's worth a try. I'm for anything that will prevent a shoot-out that can only end with at least one person dead, maybe two."

"Okay. After you finish eating and go back to town, find the kid and tell him that you talked to me. Tell him that I will be back in town around dusk and I will meet him in the Golden Nugget Saloon. We will have a drink together and come to an agreement on the rules of the gunfight."

"Rules of a gunfight?" John asked looking a bit surprised.

"Sure. You said he looked like he was new at this. Why not let him think there are rules?"

"You have got to be kidding me."

"No. If he thinks it is a lot different than in the stories he might have read about the west, he might decide this is not what he wants to do, after all."

"I think this is the strangest thing I have ever heard," John said with a grin.

"I'm sure it is, and it will be to him. We just have to convince him that gunfights in the streets of some western town are not as they appear in books and dime novels he might have read."

"Damn, Jake, you're taking an awful chance with him."

"Maybe. But if it works, we'll both be alive. If it doesn't, only one of us will be alive."

John thought about what Jake was proposing. He didn't really like the idea, but it was just crazy enough that it might work.

"Okay. We will do it your way. I should warn you that he might just be waiting for you in the Golden Nugget Saloon ready to shoot you on sight," John warned.

"I'll be ready for that," Jake said with a smile.

Nothing more was said between them while they finished eating. When they were done, John stood up, thanked Jake for dinner then walked to his horse. He swung into the saddle, then looked at Jake.

"I'll see you at the Golden Nugget Saloon around dusk," John said.

"I'll be there," Jake said as John swung his horse around and headed back toward town.

Jake watched his friend as he rode away. As soon as he was gone, Jake started cleaning up. When he was done, he poured the rest of his coffee over his fire, then made sure it was out. He packed up everything, then saddled up and headed back to Hill City.

He took his time as he thought about what might happen once he got back to town. All the way back, he thought about the kid who seemed dead set on killing him. He would have to form a plan. He would also have to be ready for anything.

Jake didn't know the kid. He wasn't sure if the kid might try to bushwhack him the minute he walked into the Golden Nugget Saloon, or maybe before he even got to the saloon.

When Jake approached the town, he swung his horse off the road and stopped. He looked down the street. There were a number of horses tied to hitching rails on both sides of the street. It seemed that everyone was in town to see if the kid was faster than the town's deputy marshal, Jake Murdock.

Jake could see the black horse standing in front of the Golden Nugget Saloon. He knew that didn't mean the kid was in the saloon. He didn't trust the kid. He turned and rode his horse around behind the buildings along the street. When Jake was about four buildings from the Golden Nugget Saloon, he stopped and stepped out of the saddle. He tied his horse to a post at the back of the general store and started walking toward the back of the saloon. As he passed between each of the buildings, he carefully checked to see if there was anyone hiding there with the idea of shooting him as he rode into town.

When he got to the last space between one of the buildings and the Golden Nugget Saloon, he saw a man kneeling behind a wood box. The man had a gun in his hand and he was peeking over the top of the box. It was obvious that he was waiting for someone. Jake was sure it was him.

Jake slowly drew his gun from his holster, then very carefully and quietly slipped up behind the man.

"Don't make a sound if you want to live," Jake said. "Drop the gun. If you make a sound, it will be the last thing you do."

The man laid the gun on the ground then put his hands on the wood box where Jake could see them. Jake stepped up closer then hit the man across the back of his head with the barrel of his gun, knocking him out cold.

Jake took the man's gun, then turned around and went to the back of the saloon. He carefully opened the backdoor and stepped inside closing the door behind him. He secured the backdoor with a hasp so no one could come in behind him. He then moved over to the door leading into the bar. He opened the door a crack and peeked out into the bar. He could see a man dressed all in black. Since he had not seen anyone dressed like that, he was sure it was the kid.

On the other side of the room sitting at a table, he could see John with a beer setting on the table in front of him. From his angle, Jake could see that John had a gun in his hand under the table. He could also see John was continually looking around the room.

"You said he would be here by dusk. It's a little later than that now," the kid said with a hint of anger in his voice.

"He will be here. I'm sure he had to clean up his fishing site," John said casually.

"I'm here," Jake said as he stepped out of the backroom into the bar.

The kid started to swing around as he reached for one of his guns.

"That would not be a good idea. You've got a table in your way and I've got a gun in my hand. I had a feeling you would try to set me up and not play by the rules. Oh, by the way, your friend is out cold next to the wood box."

The kid just sat there looking at Jake. From the way he acted and the look on his face, Jake was sure that he was very nervous, and probably scared half to death.

"What? You don't have anything to say?" Jake asked, then waited.

Jake was standing so he could see the front door of the saloon as well as the bar. While Jake glanced around the room to see if there was anyone else who might be a problem, he noticed a movement at the edge of the window next to the front door. There was someone next to the door. As the man outside looked in at the edge of the window, Jake noticed the barrel of a gun. The light next to the door had reflected off the barrel. Jake didn't hesitate, he fired a shot through the wall at the edge of the window. There was a cry of pain and someone fell on the boardwalk in front of the saloon.

Jake quickly turned and swung his gun around. Adams had decided to take the opportunity to shoot Jake, but he was too slow and not paying attention to what was around him.

Adams had barely gotten his gun up when two shots were fired at almost the same time. One shot came from Jake's gun and hit Adams square in the chest. The other shot came from under a table in the corner and hit Adams in his side just below his ribs.

All Adams had time to do was to realize that he had been shot. He died before he fell out of the chair onto the floor of the saloon.

Jake looked over at John. He was just pushing back his chair and standing up.

"Thanks for covering me," Jake said.

"I don't like back shooters."

"I'm glad of that," Jake said.

"I'll get the one next to the building," John said then turned and walked out the front of the saloon.

Jake looked around the saloon for a moment, then turned and walked out the door onto the boardwalk. The first thing he saw was two men carrying a body away. He also saw John come around the corner of the saloon. He was walking a man toward the jail. Jake followed along behind.

Jake followed John into the marshal's office and watched him lock up the man. As soon as the man was in a cell, John sat down at his desk while Jake sat down on a chair in front of it.

"I hope we don't have to go through this very often," John said.

"So do I," Jake replied.

"I sure hope things can return to normal around here."

"John, do you think I should pack up and move on?"

"Why would you do that?"

"Look what happed tonight. Some kid wanted to use me to make himself a reputation. This might not be the last time."

"First of all, I think it would be a good idea if you spent some time thinking about it. If word gets around, there may be someone else who tries. If you leave here, your reputation will go with you. All I'm saying is, take some time to think about it before you pack up and hit the trail."

"I guess you're right," Jake said thinking about it.

"I know I'm right. Now, it's time for you to get some rest. You have a job to do tomorrow. I'll see you in the morning."

"I'll see you in the morning," Jake said with a smile, then turned and left the marshal's office.

Jake went around behind the buildings and got his horse from where he had left it. He took it to the livery stable. After putting up his horse, he went to the boarding house and turned in for the night.

The next day, Jake returned to his job of helping John keep Hill City safe for its citizens. The guy they had jailed the night before, was run out of town with the warning that if he ever came back, he would be shot on sight.

CHAPTER THIRTEEN

A New Love, A New Life

Late one night, Jake was making his rounds of the bars on the main street of Hill City as usual. He was walking along the boardwalk in front of the Silver Dollar Saloon and the Golden Nugget Saloon when he heard a woman scream. He drew his pistol and stepped in between the buildings. He cautiously moved down the dark passage between the two saloons, not sure what he might find there.

When he reached the rear of the buildings, Jake caught a glimpse of someone passing by a lighted window in the back of the Silver Dollar Saloon. It was too dark to see who it was, but he was sure that it was a man.

He was about to take off after the man when he heard a soft groan off to his right. Jake turned but didn't see anyone. He took a moment to listen. When he heard the sound again, he saw where it was coming from. There in the darkness he could just barely make out a woman lying on the ground behind a firewood box. She was curled up as she clutched her stomach.

Jake slipped his gun back in his holster as he knelt down beside the woman. The first thing he noticed was her dress was torn. He gently rolled her over to get a look at her, and quickly discovered it was one of the women who worked in the Silver Dollar Saloon. He had seen her several times while making his rounds, but didn't know her name.

"Don't be afraid. It's me, Jake Murdock."

"Help me, please," she cried softly as she looked up at him.

"Where are you hurt?"

"He stabbed me."

"I'll get you to the doctor," Jake said as he bent down and picked her up.

She moaned with pain as he lifted her in his arms. Jake carried her across the street and up the stairs to the doctor's office. When he got to the door, he kicked the bottom of the door a couple of times in the hope that the doctor would be in and open the door. It took a minute or so for the doctor to get to the door and open it. As soon as the door opened, Jake pushed his way in.

"She's been stabbed, Doc," Jake said.

"Put her on the bed."

Jake placed her on the bed then stepped back. There was blood all over the front of her dress. Doc moved in close to her and started to cut her dress open to get a better look at the wound.

"How's it look?" Jake asked.

"It's not looking good. Go to the Silver Dollar Saloon and tell Kate to get up here. I'm going to need her help."

"Okay," Jake said then turned and ran out of the doctor's office.

In a matter of seconds, Jake ran into the Silver Dollar Saloon. He looked around for Kate. At first, he didn't see her. When he finally saw her, she was talking to a miner at one of the tables in a corner. He pushed his way across the room. When he came up behind her, he reached out and took her arm and turned her toward him.

"You let her go," the miner said angrily as he started to get up.

"Sorry, but I need her now," Jake said.

The miner pulled a knife out of his belt. Jake quickly drew his gun and pointed it at the miner.

"Don't do something that will get you killed," Jake said.

The miner quickly sat back down.

"Kate, one of your girls has been stabbed. Doc told me to come get you."

"Thanks," Kate said as she stepped past Jake and ran out the door of the saloon.

Jake turned around and looked at the miner. The miner had the look of fear in his eyes.

"I'm sorry Kate couldn't spend time with you right now, but one of her girls was stabbed tonight. You have any idea who might have stabbed her?"

All the miners at the table and those standing around nearby just looked at each other.

"We ain't got no idea who might want ta hurt any of the girls here," the miner who had drawn a knife said. "Which one of the girls was it?"

"I don't know her name. She's new here, but her hair is almost black and tonight she was wearing a green dress with long sleeves and white lace around the neck."

"That sounds like Maggie," one of the miners said. "She kind of a small young woman?"

"Yeah."

"That's Maggie. She's real nice. I can't think of anyone of us who would want to hurt her," another miner said.

"Did any of you see her with anybody tonight, say within the last couple of hours?"

The miners all looked at each other, then shook their heads.

"If you think of anything that might help me find out who stabbed her, let me know or tell the marshal."

The miners nodded their heads indicating that they would let him know if they remembered anything. With nothing else to do, Jake walked over to the bar to talk to the barkeeper.

"What will it be, deputy?" the barkeeper asked.

"Information. Did you see who was with Maggie this evening?"

"She was with some guy I've never seen in here before. From the looks of him, he wasn't a cowboy or a miner like we get in here most of the time. He was all duded up, sort of like one of them riverboat gamblers, if you know what I mean."

"Yeah, I get the idea. You think he might have been a gambler?"

"Could have been, but I didn't see him gamble in here."

"Was he here very long?"

"No, I don't think so," the barkeeper said thoughtfully.

"Did you see him leave?"

"I got a glimpse of him just as he walked out the door, but I didn't see if he was with anyone. He could have been."

"Did you see Maggie after he left?"

The barkeeper thought for a moment, then said, "I can't say for sure. It was kind of busy earlier. I sure wish I could be more help. Sorry. There is one thing that might help if you're looking for the duded-up fella."

"What's that?

"He was wearing a light colored, maybe gray, flat crowned and flat brimmed hat with a silver hatband, and a dark coat over a white shirt. I ain't never seen a hat like that around here before."

"Thanks," Jake said then turned and walked out of the Silver Dollar Saloon.

Jake stopped on the boardwalk of the saloon and looked up and down the street. Since the man he saw running behind the building had headed north, he decided he would start by walking north and check all the bars and brothels toward that end of town.

The first place he came to was a brothel, he stepped inside and asked the madam about the man he was looking for. She told him there had been a man dressed like that in her place, but he left over an hour ago.

Jake left and continued down the street stopping in each saloon and brothel along the way. By the time he got to the end of the street, several saloons had told him that the man had stopped in, looked around then left without talking to anyone.

With no success in finding the man, he started south from the north end of town on the other side of the street. Jake had gone to several saloons and brothels on his way back. It wasn't long and he ran into John.

"Hi, what's going on? I've seen you going from one bar to the next like you're looking for someone." John said.

"I'm looking for a guy wearing a dark coat over a white shirt, and a light colored gray hat with a flat brim and crown, and silver hatband."

"What do you want him for?"

"He knifed one of the girls that works in the Silver Dollar. At least, he was the last person seen with the girl."

"Who'd he knife?"

"The new girl. I think her name is Maggie. She's over at Doc's office. It's not looking good for her."

"Dressed like that, he should be easy to spot. Have you checked in the hotels? He might be staying there."

"No, not yet."

"Okay. You finish checking out the saloons and brothels. I'll check out the hotels," John said. "If we don't find him, we will meet back at the office. If you find him, arrest him. We'll find out if he is the one who knifed her."

"Okay."

Jake had searched for the man with the gray hat until all the brothels and saloons had been checked out. He had not found the man. It was as if he had disappeared into thin air.

As soon as Jake was done, he went to the marshal's office hoping that John might have found out something. When he walked in the door, he saw John sitting behind his desk. Jake sat down in a chair in front of the desk and let out a sigh of disappointment.

"I take it you didn't have any luck in finding the man with the gray hat?" John asked.

"No. He just disappeared. No one seems to know who he was, or why he was here."

"I don't think there is anything more we can do tonight. I think we should turn in for the night and pick it up in the morning," John said.

"I think I'll stop off at Doc's office and see how Maggie is doing."

John just nodded then stood up. He followed Jake out the door then stood on the boardwalk and watched Jake as he walked toward Doc's office. When Jake turned to go up the stairs to Doc's office, John turned and went in the other direction toward his home.

Jake went up the stairs and knocked on the door to Doc's office. It was answered by Kate. Jake stepped inside and looked across the room at the bed where Maggie laid.

"How is she doing?"

"It wasn't as bad as Doc first thought. She will be laid up for a while, but she'll recover."

"Where's Doc?"

"He's resting in the other room. I'm to call him when she wakes up."

"Would you like me to stay with her? I know you've put in a long day," Jake said.

"So have you. Did you find who did this to her?"

"I'm afraid not. It seems he just disappeared. Go get some rest. I'll watch over her for now. You can relieve me in the morning," Jake suggested. "Besides, I can't sleep now anyway."

"Okay, but call Doc if you get too sleepy or she wakes up."

"I will."

As Kate left the doctor's office, Jake pulled up a chair next to the bed. He watched Maggie for several minutes. She seemed to be resting peacefully.

Jake leaned back in the chair and began to think about what had happened. His head filled with questions. Why did the man in the gray hat attack Maggie? What did he hope to gain? How did he disappear so quickly? Did he leave town, or had he simply changed clothes so he would not be recognized?

The questions running through his mind were not getting answered. They were unlikely to get answered until Maggie could talk to him. However, the one thought that seemed to stick in Jake's mind was why did the man attack Maggie? She was new in town. She hadn't been in Hill City more than a week, eight or nine days at the most. Did her attacker know her from someplace else? Did she do something to him that caused him to attack her? These were all good questions, but what were the answers? Jake had no answers. Since the man appeared to have gone from one saloon to the next, he must have been looking for her.

Jake tried to change his train of thought. He began to think about where the man in the gray hat had gone. The best answer to that was to track him. If Jake could pick up the tracks from behind the saloon, he might find out where he went. He decided that in the morning he would go to where Maggie had been stabbed and look for tracks. It was too dark to do anything about it now.

Jake slouched down in the chair and leaned back. It wasn't long and he was asleep. He woke several times during the night when he heard Maggie move slightly in the bed.

When morning came, Jake woke to the sound of someone coming into the room. He opened his eyes, turned around in the chair and saw Doc.

"Did you spend the whole night in that chair," Doc asked.

"Yeah."

"You can go now. Get some coffee and a good breakfast," Doc said.

Jake stood up and stretched. He was a little stiff.

"That sounds like a good idea. I'll stop in later," Jake said.

Doc simply nodded at Jake. As soon as Jake had gone, Doc walked up to Maggie. He lifted the blanket off Maggie and checked the wound to make sure it was doing well. He laid the blanket back over her then went to his desk and sat down.

After Jake left Doc's office, he walked across the street. He stepped up on the boardwalk then walked down the street to the boarding house where he was staying. Jake went inside and had breakfast.

As soon as he finished breakfast, he went up to his room. He washed his face and put on a clean shirt then left the boarding house.

Instead of walking along the boardwalk in front of the businesses, he walked around behind the two saloons to the place where he had found Maggie. Jake immediately began looking for any kind of tracks that might give him some idea where her attacker might have gone. The ground near where he found Maggie showed a lot of scuffling. It was apparent that Maggie had struggled with her attacker. The only clear tracks were his after he picked her up and took her to Doc's office.

Jake remembered that he had seen someone behind the building next to where he found her. He walked over to where he had seen the man last night. He found several clear prints in the dirt just below the window. One of the footprints showed the man was wearing shoes, not boots. The indentation just in front of the heel of the shoe showed the man was wearing something on his shoes. Since they were shoes not boots, Jake wondered if the man was wearing spats. No one would notice the spats because they would be covered by his pant legs. He could not think of anyone in town who wore shoes and spats.

Looking at the footprints, Jake began to follow them. The footprints went as far as the next building and disappeared at the backdoor. Jake looked up at the building. It was easy for him to figure out that it was a brothel owned by one Julius McMorris, a man who had made it clear that he was going to run his business his way, regardless of the laws of Hill City.

Jake knew that Julius had had words with John sometime ago when John threatened to close him down if he didn't follow the law. As far as Jake knew, Julius had reluctantly complied but only after John had shut him down a couple of times. Even then it was not without a lot of grumbling and complaining.

Since Jake had seen very little of McMorris, he had no idea how he dressed. It seemed to Jake that McMorris would be the type of man who would wear spats, but he could not remember ever seeing him wearing spats or a gray flat brimmed hat. If he remembered correctly, McMorris had been a riverboat gambler some years ago. Rumor had it he had made his money gambling. It was also rumored that he had several women who would provide services for the men who had beat him at cards. It was said that the women would sleep with the winners, then steal their money while the winners slept it off, and leave the boat before the men woke up. It was also said that he was tossed off several riverboats for cheating.

The question that came to Jake's mind was why would McMorris attack Maggie? As he thought about his question, he pictured McMorris in his mind. The man he saw behind the brothel was too tall and slim to be McMorris, but he went in the backdoor.

Jake knew that there were a number of local married men who would visit the brothels. They would use the backdoors in order to avoid anyone seeing them go inside. He knew it was possible that the man he saw had nothing to do with the stabbing. However, he might know who did. It was time to go have a talk with McMorris, not that he expected him to be of any help.

Jake went around to the front of the brothel and walked in. There were several women who were dressed rather scantily sitting in a room waiting for someone to come to use their services. One of the women stood up and walked over to Jake.

"Do you see anything you like, Deputy?" she asked as she opened her thin robe to reveal the fact that she was wearing a very thin nightgown that showed she had nothing on under it.

"No. I want to talk to McMorris."

"Oh," she said with a hint of disappointment as she pulled the robe closed.

"Is he here?"

"Mr. McMorris is in his office," she said and pointed to a door in the back of the room.

Jake just nodded then walked up to the door. He thought he could hear voices inside the office. He reached out and knocked on the door.

"Who is it?"

"Deputy Murdock. I would like to speak with you for a moment."

There was silence for a moment, but Jake thought he heard a backdoor close just seconds before the door to McMorris's office opened. McMorris was standing in the doorway.

"What do you want?" McMorris asked rather sharply.

"I think it would be better if we talk in private."

McMorris hesitated for a moment then stepped back so Jake could enter his office. Once inside, Jake looked around. There was no one there, but he looked down at the floor and saw muddy tracks that were made by shoes. He had seen where someone had stepped in a place near the corner of the building where Jake had noticed the ground was wet when he was out behind the building.

"Who just left your office?"

"That's none of your business."

"I'm looking for the man that made the muddy tracks on your carpet. Who is he and where did he go?" Jake demanded.

"That is none of your business."

"I'm making it my business. Why did you have Maggie attacked last night? By the way, whoever did it didn't do a very good job of it. She is going to live and tell me who attacked her."

"She doesn't know," McMorris said with a slight grin.

"But you do," Jake said while looking into his eyes.

Jake could see the change in McMorris. The look of confidence in his eyes was gone. He was a little nervous.

"You hired someone to attack her, why?"

"By the time you find out you'll be dead," McMorris said harshly.

Jake drew his gun and pointed it right at McMorris's gut. McMorris took a step back.

"We're going to take a little walk over to the marshal's office. We'll finish this conversation while you are in jail."

Keeping his gun pointed at McMorris's belly, Jake reached out and took McMorris's gun from inside his coat. After slipping the gun in his belt, Jake motioned for McMorris to start for the door.

"If you try anything, I'll put a hole in that fancy suit you're wearing."

Jake followed closely behind McMorris as they walked to the front of the building. At the front door, Jake had McMorris stop. Jake looked out but didn't see anyone.

"You will turn down the boardwalk until we are straight across the street from the jail. We will then cross the street. One mistake and it will be the last one you make. Now start moving."

Jake followed McMorris out onto the boardwalk. He stayed very close to his prisoner. They passed one gap between buildings very carefully. All was going well, but they still had a ways to go.

Suddenly, there was a scream from behind Jake. He quickly turned, pulling McMorris in front of him. As he turned, two shots were fired at him. One of the shots hit Jake before he could shoot back. He fell on the boardwalk and rolled off into the dirt. The other shot hit McMorris in the gut. He collapsed on the boardwalk.

Jake laid in the dirt in pain. The shot had hit him on the top of his hip. It was very painful but not life threatening. As the shock of being hit wore off, he looked up. He could see a man walking toward him with a gun in his hand. It was the same man he had seen in the alley behind the Silver Dollar Saloon.

Jake could see his gun lying on the boardwalk where it fell from his hand when he was shot. He knew if he didn't do something quickly, the man was going to kill him.

Out of nowhere, Jake heard the marshal yell at the man to drop the gun. When the man turned to shoot the marshal, Jake grabbed the gun he had stuck in his belt. He wasted no time in shooting the man, dropping him dead in the street.

As John came running to Jake's aid. Jake heard McMorris call out to the man lying dead in the street.

"Eric. Eric," McMorris called out, but Eric didn't move.

Jake tried to stand but was unable with the injury to his hip. He pulled himself up on the boardwalk and looked at McMorris. It was easy to see that McMorris was in pain.

204

McMorris turned and looked at Jake and said, "You - - killed - - my - - son," then he coughed and collapsed on the boardwalk. He was dead.

Jake turned and looked at John. He could see the worried look in John's eyes.

"I guess I'll be laid up for awhile," Jake said.

"I guess you will. Come on, I'll get you over to Doc's."

A couple of locals were standing nearby watching John help Jake stand up. John looked at them.

"Get those bodies off the street," John said.

John turned and helped Jake to the doctor's office while the men took the bodies to the undertaker. Once Jake's injury had been cleaned, stitched up and a clean dressing put on it by Doc, he helped Jake to the sofa where he was instructed to stay.

"You're going be laid up for awhile. You have to stay off your feet for six days, and to make sure you do, I will be keeping you here. If you don't obey my instructions, I'll have John lock you up for those few days," Doc said. "I don't want you opening that wound."

"I'll watch over him," a female voice said softly.

Jake turned and looked at Maggie. She was sitting up a little in the bed in the corner. He smiled at her.

"It's the least I could do for someone who saved my life and watched over me all night," Maggie said.

"I won't have any problem staying right here," Jake said as he looked at Maggie.

During the long days of resting in the doctor's office, Jake and Maggie talked. Maggie told him about Eric McMorris wanting her, but she didn't like him. She moved to Hill City hoping he would not be able to find her. She didn't know that Eric's father had a saloon and brothel in Hill City until after she moved.

They also talked about what they wanted for the future. It seemed that neither of them wanted the jobs they had.

The more they shared their feelings and desires for the future, the closer they became.

On the day that Jake was released from the doctor's office, he limped over to the marshal's office. John was sitting behind his desk when Jake walked in.

"Well, it's good to see you getting around. From the way you're walking, I doubt you are ready to return to work."

"I'm thinking about not coming back to work."

"Oh. What are you going to do?"

"There's a place just west of Custer on the edge of the Black Hills that I have had an eye on for some time. I've got some money saved up, enough to buy the land and get a few head of cattle, even enough for a few chickens, and a couple of workhorses."

"So, you're going to become a cattleman?"

"Yeah," Jake said with a grin. "I've always had that in the back of my mind. Now seems to be a good time to do it."

"There wouldn't happen to be a young lady that feels the same way, would there?" John asked with a grin.

"Yeah," Jake said. "As soon as the doctor releases her we are going to get married and move out to the ranch. We'll live in a tent while we build a cabin."

"I will miss you around here, but I'm happy for you. By the way, I have a bank draft for you from a bank in Cheyenne, Wyoming," John said as he reached in the draw of his desk.

"It's the reward for capturing Eric McMorris, two thousand dollars. He was wanted dead or alive. He had killed two people in the bank. This should help you get a good start on your ranch."

"I guess this will be my last bounty check," Jake said with a big grin. "I'm done bounty hunting."

"Glad to hear it," John said as he stood up.

John reached out and shook Jake's hand. Jake didn't know what to say so he turned around and left the marshal's office.

Four days later, Maggie was released from Doc's care. Two days later, Maggie and Jake were married. John stood up for Jake, and Kate stood up for Maggie.

After the wedding, they said goodbye to their friends and left Hill City in a small wagon that Jake had bought. They bought the land west of Custer City and several head of cattle. They worked hard together to build a ranch and a life for themselves.

CHAPTER FOURTEEN

No peace for a bounty hunter

Time had passed with Maggie and Jake spending their days working on their ranch. They had built a barn with the help of several neighbors, a corral where Jake could train horses and a cabin only about thirty feet from a creek.

The bull they purchased the year before had done his job well. In the pasture were twenty new calves just starting to eat the grass that was abundant on the ranch.

All had been going well for the young couple as they worked hard to make their ranch a success. That was until three men came riding up to the cabin.

Jake was out by the barn working with a young horse. It was a brown and white paint he had bought from an Indian for Maggie.

Jake had seen the three riders come down the lane toward their cabin. He noticed that they were well armed and looked like they had been riding for some distance. He didn't like the looks of them. A vision of him finding his parents on his return from town several years ago to find his parents murdered by three men came to his mind. He wasn't about to let that happen again. Jake ducked into the barn and picked up his rifle, then moved close to the barn door where he could watch them.

The three riders stopped in front of the cabin. Maggie stepped outside, leaving the door to the cabin open.

"Howdy, Ma'am. We saw the name "Murdock" on the gate. We're looking for a man by the name of Jake Murdock. Would this happen to be his spread?"

Maggie could see past the man. She saw Jake in the barn with a rifle. He was shaking his head in an effort to get her to tell them he was not at home.

"Yes, it is, but he is not here right now."

"Do you know where he is?"

"He went to town. Why do you ask?"

"Do you know when he'll be back?" the man asked, ignoring her question.

"No, but he should be back by dark."

The man looked at her of a moment then turned to the other two men. He didn't say anything to the other two for a moment, then turned back and looked at Maggie again."

"Ma'am, I don't believe you. I think you best tell me where he is."

Maggie just looked at the man. She wasn't sure what she should do, until the man started to get off his horse. She quickly turned and ran into the cabin slamming the door behind her.

The man's foot no more than touched the ground when a shot was fired from the barn. The shot Jake fired hit the man in the leg causing him to fall to the ground. It also frightened the horses. The horse bucked a couple of times then ran off leaving its rider lying in the dirt.

The other two men jumped off their horses and ran for cover. One of them ran over to a watering trough and dove down behind it. He began shooting toward the barn from behind the trough.

The other one ran around to the side of the cabin. He began shooting at the barn from the cover of the cabin.

Maggie ran to the bedroom where there was a shotgun next to the bed. Maggie grabbed it and ran back to a window. She could see the one man lying on the ground holding his leg, but she couldn't see the other two men from inside the cabin. She heard the sound of gunshots that came from the side of the cabin and from the watering trough. Several gunshots came from near the barn which assured her that Jake was still putting up a fight.

It wasn't but a few minutes and the shooting stopped. After a few minutes more, Jake came out of the barn. He was being very cautious and looking off toward the watering trough.

Lying next to the watering trough was a man. He had a hole in his head. Jake quickly looked around for the last of the three men.

As Jake moved closer to a stack of hay, Maggie stepped out of the cabin with the shotgun in her hands. She noticed the first man to be shot was reaching for his gun. Without any hesitation, Maggie swung the shotgun around and pulled the trigger. The shotgun went off just as the injured man tried to shoot Jake. The blast from the shotgun killed the man instantly.

Jake quickly turned and saw Maggie with the shotgun. Maggie had saved his life, but it wasn't over. There was one other man. Jake looked back at the corner of the cabin where he had last seen the last of the three men.

The third man came out from behind the corner of the cabin on the other side of it. Jake heard him and turned around just as the man grabbed Maggie from behind. He held her in front of him as a shield to keep Jake from shooting at him. He held his gun against Maggie's head.

"Drop the gun or I'll kill her," he yelled at Jake.

Instead of dropping the rifle, Jake slowly raised it up and aimed it right at the man's head.

"I said drop the gun," the third man said nervously.

"You are not going to get out of here alive. If you kill her, I'll kill you."

Jake could see that the man was thinking about his position. Jake was also close enough that he would be able to kill the man if he was given even the slightest chance.

"If I let her go, you will kill me anyway," the man said.

Jake was just waiting for him to make one little mistake, one mistake that would give Jake the opening to kill him without Maggie getting hurt.

Suddenly, the man moved the barrel away from Maggie's head and started to swing it so it would be pointed at Jake. Maggie dropped to the ground causing the man to take his eyes off Jake and lose his balance for just a second. At that moment Jake fired, his bullet hit the man in the head. As the man fell to the ground, his gun went off, the bullet hit Jake in the leg causing Jake to fall to the ground.

Maggie got up and ran to Jake's aid. She helped him to his feet and into the cabin where she treated his wound. Once his wound was treated, she looked up at him.

"What are we going to do? How can we live in peace with people coming here to kill you?"

Jake looked at her. He didn't answer her right away. He thought about what she had said, and she was right. He didn't want her to have to live like that; never knowing when someone would come by the ranch to make a reputation for himself by being the one who killed Jake Murdock, a man known to be fast with a gun. Jake came up with a plan. He looked at Maggie and smiled.

"I have a plan," Jake said. "But first, I want to know if you want to sell this place and move someplace else?"

Maggie thought for a moment before she answered.

"I really like this place; but if moving would make us safe from attacks like this one, yes, I would be willing to move. But I don't see how moving would change anything. They will find us and try to kill you. We would end up having to move again and again, until someone kills you," she said almost in tears, knowing it would do no good to move.

"I think I know a way we can stay here."

"How? How can we possibly stay here?"

"The first thing is to dig a grave and put a marker on the grave with my name on it and the date of my death, today's date. Then we need to get the three men who came here loaded across their horses. You will take them into town and tell the sheriff that they attacked us and killed me."

"But won't he think it a little strange that all three were killed by you?"

"No, not since you killed one with a shotgun."

"I hadn't thought about that," Maggie said suddenly realizing what Jake was thinking.

"Anyway, I will stay out of sight until I can grow a full beard and mustache, and let my hair grow longer, probably about four to six months. I will have a limp from this wound for a long time," he added.

"When my beard and hair have grown out, I will reappear as someone else. We'll get married again using a new name. Then we'll put our new name on the front gate, and you and I will continue to ranch without anyone knowing," he explained. "What do you think?"

Maggie looked at him for a moment then began to smile.

"What about our neighbors? Do you think they will say anything?" she asked.

"I doubt it. Besides they all live some distance away. By the time they find out that I was killed, I will not look like I do now."

"Do you think it will work?" Maggie asked.

"I think it's worth a try. We'll have to be careful not to let on that I'm still alive. How would you like me with a new name?"

"As long as it's still you, I don't care what your name is," she said, then leaned down and kissed him.

"I think we should get started. The first thing we have to do is get those men on their horses."

"You can't be lifting them up. You'll open your wound," Maggie said.

"Tie a cloth tight around my leg, tight enough so I can't bend my leg. Then help me up."

"Can we wait till morning? I will need time to mourn my loss," Maggie said. "It will also give you a chance to rest a little."

"That's a good idea.

"I'll go get their horses and put them in the corral," Maggie said.

"Okay."

Jake laid in the bed and watched as Maggie left the cabin. He thought about his plan while she was gone. He wasn't sure that it would work, but it was the best idea he could come up with. If it did work, they could live in peace. If it didn't work, they would have to move to someplace where he was not known and live under a different name.

After Maggie had put the horses in the corral, she fixed dinner. After dinner, Jake fell asleep on the bed while Maggie cleaned up the dishes.

Jake woke with Maggie lying beside him. He turned and looked at her only to find her looking back at him.

"You just lay there. I'll fix breakfast. After breakfast we will do what we have to do," she said.

After breakfast Maggie checked the dressing on Jake's leg. Satisfied that it was tight, she helped him up. He leaned on her as they went outside. As soon as he was ready, they walked up to the first body.

"I'll wait here. Get one of the horses," Jake said.

Maggie walked over to the corral, took the reins of one of the horses and led the horse over next to the dead man. Between the two of them, they were able to get the man over the saddle, then Maggie tied the man to the saddle. She then led the horse to the hitching rail in front of the cabin.

It was slow going, but Maggie and Jake were able to get the other two men over the backs of their horses in the same way. When they were done, Maggie tied the three horses together.

Once the horses were ready to go, Maggie went to the barn and saddled a horse. She led it to the front of the cabin and tied it to the hitching rail. She turned and looked at Jake.

"What about a grave for you? If the sheriff wants to come back with me, he'll probably want to see where you are buried."

"It will probably take you the rest of the day to get to town, talk to the sheriff and get back here. I'll fix up a place that will look like a grave while you are gone. Over by that tree the ground is fairly soft, that would make a good place for a grave," he said as he pointed to a lone tree on a little rise off to the east. "I'll put the grave there. That way you will be able to tell the sheriff where you buried me."

"Okay, but take it easy on the leg. Take time to rest it."

"I will. You better get going."

Maggie stepped in front of Jake, then rose up on her tiptoes and kissed him. He held her for a minute before he let her go. Jake watched her as she swung into the saddle of her horse. She took hold of the reins of the lead horse, looked over her shoulder at Jake, then turned back around and led the horses down the lane to the road. Jake stood watching her until she was out of sight and on her way to Custer City.

As soon as she was out of sight, Jake hobbled over to the barn and got a shovel. He hobbled to the spot he had pointed out to Maggie where he dug a hole about the size of a grave for someone his size. He returned to the barn and sat down to rest.

After resting for about thirty minutes, he saddled a horse then got an old blanket. He led the horse out to where he had stacked some logs he planned to cut up for the winter. Jake picked out a log about six foot long, tied a rope around it then tied the end of the rope to the saddle. He led the horse to the grave site, untied the log then rolled it into the grave. He put a blanket over the log, tucked it under the log, then filled the grave with the dirt. He smoothed it out, then patted it down with the shovel. He brushed out the drag marks made by the log. When he was finished, he stood back and looked at the grave. He was satisfied that it looked like a fresh grave.

Jake returned to the barn, unsaddled the horse and let it loose in the corral. He went into the cabin and laid down. Jake checked his leg. Jake had not opened the wound. The bandage had been tight enough to prevent the wound from opening. It took him a long time to get to sleep as the stress he had put on his injured leg had caused it to be very painful.

After resting for a couple of hours, Jake got up and walked out to the barn. He climbed up into the hayloft and laid down while he waited for Maggie to return.

It was mid-afternoon, about three o'clock, when Jake heard horses coming up the lane toward the cabin from the road. He looked out the loft door and could see Maggie and Sheriff Metcalf coming toward the cabin. They had in tow the three horses that had belonged to the three men who had attacked them. They rode up to the barn and led the horses into the corral.

Sheriff Metcalf stepped out of the saddle and tied his horse to the top rail of the corral. Maggie did the same.

"I want to thank you for your help," Maggie said.

"Think nothing of it. Jake helped me when I needed it. I'll help you unsaddle the horses?"

"Shouldn't you have kept the horses?" she asked as Sheriff Metcalf walked into the corral.

"You deserve them. If you don't need them, you can sell them. I'm sure a little extra money will come in handy. It will help pay for a ranch hand to help out until you decide what you want to do."

"I plan to stay right here," Maggie said.

While they talked, the sheriff took the saddles off the horses and carried them into the barn. He put them over the top board of one of the stalls.

"Shouldn't you take the saddlebags back to town?"

"I don't have any use for them, and they certainly don't have any use for them now. Who knows. There might be something in them you can use."

Maggie looked at the saddles and saddlebags. She had no idea what the men would have had in their saddlebags that she could use.

"I best be going back to town. I'll file a claim for the reward on the men. When I get it, I'll bring it out to you. The reward should be enough to help pay for a ranch hand or two for at least a couple of years."

"Thank you. I'm sure Jake would have wanted me to have it so I could keep the ranch."

"I'm sure he would," Sheriff Metcalf said then swung up into the saddle.

Maggie stood next to the corral and watched as Sheriff Metcalf turned his horse and started down the lane to the road.

"That was nice of Metcalf to give you the horses," Jake said from the loft.

"I didn't invite him into the cabin for coffee because I thought you might be in the cabin."

"It's okay."

"I was ready to show him where I buried you if he asked. You did get a grave dug?"

"Yes, I did. The only thing left to do is to put a grave marker on the grave and for us to decide on a new name. What would you like for a new name?" Jake asked.

"We can't use my maiden name because it is on our marriage certificate. I have an idea for a name."

"What do you have in mind?"

"Does anyone know your mother's maiden name?"

"No, I don't think so," Jake said.

"What was her maiden name?"

"Peterson, Millie Peterson."

"If you use her maiden name, you would already have a family history," Maggie suggested.

"Okay. How does Jacob Peterson sound?"

"It sounds good to me. Now all you have to do is grow a beard, mustache and longer hair," Maggie said with a grin.

"I'll have to stay out of sight for a few months, then show up and you can hire me as a ranch hand," Jake said.

"I'll hire you for more than that," Maggie said as she stepped up to him.

She put her arms around his neck, raised up on her toes and kissed him hard. Jake held her tightly as he returned her kiss.

After several months, they decided that Jake no longer looked the same with his long hair and thick dark beard and mustache. Jake rode around so he came into Custer City from the east side of town. He rode into town as Jacob Peterson.

It was going to be his first test to see if anyone recognized him. If Sheriff Metcalf didn't recognize him, there was a very good chance no one else would. With the change in his appearance and the limp from the gunshot wound to his leg, he felt he was ready. Jacob went to the sheriff's office. He found Metcalf sitting behind his desk.

"Excuse me, sir, my name's Jacob Peterson. I'm lookin' for a job. Do you happen to know anyone around here who might be lookin' for someone who's a pretty good ranch hand? I know how to work with horses and cattle. I can fix about anything. I know I've got a limp, but I can do just about anything."

"Where are you from?"

"Up north. I worked on a ranch over near Belle Fourche. I got let go when the owner died in an accident and his son took over. He let me go cause of my game leg, but I can do about anything any cowboy can do," Jacob said as he pleaded his case.

"The only person I know looking for a ranch hand is a widow lady east of here. It's the Murdock Ranch."

"You think she might hire a man with a limp?"

"I don't know, but she would probably give you a try. Just go west about six miles. You'll see the name on the gate."

"Thank you, sir," Jacob said. "Thank you. I'll head out that way and talk to her."

Jacob left the sheriff's office glad that Metcalf had not recognized him. He returned to the ranch and told Maggie about what had happened at the sheriff's office.

After almost a year, Jacob and Maggie rode into Custer City where they were married. When they returned to the ranch, they changed the name at the front gate. It was now Peterson's Ranch. Jacob and Maggie spent their remaining years as Mr. and Mrs. Jacob Peterson. They raised a lot of cattle and a couple of children on their ranch west of Custer City without any troubles related to their past.